MAFIA LOVE

THE ACCIDENTAL MAFIA QUEEN BOOK 3

KHARDINE GRAY

Copyright © 2019 by Khardine Gray

Mafia Love Copyright © 2019 by Khardine Gray

All rights reserved.

Cover design © 2019 by Cover by Combs

Photography- Eric Battershell Photography

Cover Model - Johnny Kane

Editing : Julia Goda : Diamond In the Rough Editing

This work is copyrighted. Apart from any use as permitted under the Copyright Act 1968, no part may be reproduced, copied, scanned, stored in a retrieval system, recorded or transmitted, in any form or by any means, without the prior written permission of the author, except for the use of brief quotations in a book review.

This is a work of fiction. Names, characters, businesses, places, events and incidents are either the products of the author's imagination or used in a fictitious manner. Any resemblance to actual persons, living or dead, or actual events is purely coincidental.

The author asserts that all characters and situations depicted in this work of fiction are entirely imaginary and bear no relation to any real person.

No part of this book may be reproduced in any form or by any electronic or mechanical means, including information storage and retrieval systems, without written permission from the author, except for the use of brief quotations in a book review.

The following story contains mature themes, strong language and sexual situations.

It is intended for mature readers. All characters are 18+ years of age and all sexual acts are consensual.

MAFIA LOVE

USA TODAY BESTSELLING AUTHOR
Khardine Gray

MAFIA QUOTE

" Friendship is everything. Friendship is more than talent. It is more than the government. It is almost the equal of family." – The Godfather

CHAPTER 1

Amelia

Arabesque, pirouette, pirouette, glissade and a hop. That was it.

Then on my toes, arms out, head up and four skips into a leap.

That leap... Wow, I caught a glimpse of myself in the mirrors as I flew through the air and landed on the tips of my toes. I hardly looked any different to what I was years ago. I didn't look any different to who I used to be.

"Dance, Amelia," Dad called with laughter and pride in his voice.

And that was the moment I let go and truly unlocked myself.

The music took me, and I just went with it.

Jumping and spinning, flowing as if I weighed nothing, flying through the air.

When the music stopped, several people were clapping and I almost believed I was back at the performance for real.

My hand flew up to my cheeks when I saw both Luc and Millicent standing by the door.

Luc.

I moved to run to him, to throw myself into his arms and savor the euphoria that rippled through me at having been able to dance again.

But I stopped and turned to my father, who was beaming at me with a smile full of love and adoration.

I rushed up to him instead and hugged him.

"Thank you," he whispered into my ear.

"No, thank you."

He smiled down at me, then glanced at Luc, inclining his head toward him. "Go, go be with your guy. Have some normal if only for a few hours more."

Normal.

Yes. I turned to go to Luc and skipped into his

arms, giving Millicent a bright smile as I approached.

Alarms sounded just before I reached Luc, stopping me in my tracks.

What was that?

"Someone's in the house," Dad called out.

"You said the security was turned off." I winced turning back to him.

"It is. This is a homemade trip wire I placed in the library."

"What's in the library?" Luc asked.

I looked back to him. "The safe." My heart squeezed.

"What's in the safe, Amelia?"

I looked to Dad before confirming that, and he nodded. "The key to the diamonds." We'd put it there yesterday.

"Fuck. Stay here."

Dad was already moving past us. Luc rested a hand on him to hold him back.

"Stay, Raphael."

"This is my home. How dare they come in here," Dad snarled.

"Mr. Rossi, please," Millicent offered. "Please stay, you... aren't well."

Beads of sweat formed on her upper lip.

Strange because it wasn't exactly hot in here. Must be the anxiety. I felt that too.

I moved past Luc and Dad.

"Amelia, you stay here with your father and Millicent."

"No, I won't stay. We go together."

"Remember what happened when you—"

I didn't allow him to finish. I moved on ahead of him through the door. He followed me and took hold of my arm to pull me back.

"Jesus, Amelia, don't you understand I'm trying to keep you safe?"

"Yes. I do. I understand, but you know I'm not useless. I want to see who this person is."

"Stay beside me and don't break away. Stay with me."

"I will," I assured him.

From his back pocket he whipped out a gun and handed it to me. He then took out his gun from his side pocket and held it up ready to fire.

Like I'd promised, I stayed beside him, and we proceeded up the steps and on to the second floor, where the library was situated.

Who could it be?

Who was it?

And... how did they know to go to the library?

How the fuck would they have known that? It

was just Dad and me talking that day in the garden. There'd been no one else.

No one saw me when I went to the library. I'd made sure of it.

I heard shuffling in there as we approached and books being thrown around.

"How the fuck hard can it be to find a safe?" came a voice I recognized well.

It couldn't be.

Luc and I walked into the library and saw not only Jefferson but Holloway inside.

They stopped throwing the books from the shelf and turned to meet our gazes.

"Well, well, well. I see we just discovered who the rats are," Luc mused, pointing his gun at them. "Not one but two of them. Vermin. Fucking vermin."

My mouth and throat were dry.

Shock flew through me. Shock and surprise, tangled with betrayal. More betrayal. I would never have guessed it was them.

It was fine for Luc; he didn't know them like I did. I thought they were my friends.

But then I guess I was kidding myself.

I didn't know them at all.

Jefferson and Holloway. My God.

They were my enemies.

I swallowed hard, but I couldn't get past the lump in my throat.

I just couldn't believe what I was seeing before me, but really, why should I be so surprised?

Luc didn't appear shocked at all. He'd known it was them. Surely, he must have known it was one of them.

But both?

Jefferson and Holloway came as a duo. They'd been friends as far back as I could remember and did everything together. They were the kind of friends who followed each other for good or bad. So, if one was a rat, the other was tainted too.

Didn't make it any easier though. It didn't. They were my friends. Guys I would have trusted with my life.

"Why... *why?*" The words fell from my lips straight from the wound of betrayal. I shook my head at them.

Jefferson had the audacity to smile at me. He had the audacity to look at me and smile, like this was nothing. It made me feel like throwing up.

"Nothing personal, Taylor, or should I say Rossi?" He smirked.

Holloway stood in that casual manner he usually exuded. They hadn't pulled their guns yet. Why?

"Nothing personal? Really? We were friends. Sinclaire could have died." When I thought of all that had happened, my soul ached, and I had to fight to keep from crumbling inside. I had to fight my emotions that tore at me the more it sunk in that they were involved.

"Sinclaire is a fool in love with you." Holloway laughed.

Out the corner of my eye I noticed how Luc tensed at the mention of that. Looked like everyone could see how deeply Sinclaire cared for me long before I did.

"So, he deserved to die?"

"He was in the way."

Luc raised his gun higher. "Cut the shit. How'd you get in the house? How'd you know to come in here?"

That was the important stuff, but I had so many questions I wanted to ask.

"Instructions from our boss," Jefferson answered.

"What boss?" I had to ask. I had to know how this whole thing unraveled and led to me. It was vague in my mind, and maybe I didn't need specifics, but I sure as fuck wanted to know how these people got to my friends and what price they put on my head to lure them to the dark side.

"Typical Amelia Taylor. She wants to know why."

"Tell her," Luc cut in, his voice taking on an edge I'd never heard.

Jefferson laughed. "Sure thing. Months ago, we were approached with an offer. We both got a phone call each. No name, just a muffled voice. The guy offered us ten grand each if we could give him access to our staff database. Of course, we did it, and they fixated on you. After that, we were offered a million each to work with them. An irrefusable offer. It took a while, but from some old hospital records they had on you, they were able to get access to your DNA files, but it was inconclusive. Inconclusive with a trail, though, because they noticed a glitch in your listing on the system. It was a dead giveaway that something had been changed. That was actually what highlighted you. This guy has friends in high places, but looks like Don Raphael has the same kinds of friends, too, because they couldn't match out your identity. They tried to take you several times. It was actually me who suggested they do it the old-fashioned straightforward way and take your hairbrush and lipstick. That was all they needed to confirm their theory of you being the secret daughter of the head of the Chicago mafia. We were shocked to shit when we found out."

So, that was it.

"Good, story over." Luc spoke the minute Jefferson finished and without warning fired a shot straight into his arm.

Holloway sprang into action, whipping out his gun, taken by surprise. Luc shoved me out of the way as Jefferson went after me.

When shots were fired, I dove behind the desk, but Holloway came after me. I never expected him to. He just went for me.

"Can't get the key, so I'll grab the next prize," he taunted.

I jumped out of the way when he tried to grab me and sent a kick straight to his chest. He stumbled, stunned by my sudden motion, but regained his balance.

Holloway had that built that made you easily mistake him for being less tough, but he had muscle and speed. His thin presence was more athletic than on the lanky side, which gave him the advantage. Being used to him, I knew that.

I straightened, raised my gun, but damn, he sent a punch to my hand and knocked it out. Shit,

I needed to focus because he could take me down now if he wanted to. He was taller than me and stronger. He also knew me too. We'd been on so many raids and other encounters where we'd had to fight.

Luc and Jefferson were on the floor now. Fists were flying. Luc looked like he was winning, but I couldn't focus on him. Holloway dove for me again. This time he got me. He grabbed me and squeezed my ribs hard to the point where I thought I'd pass out. I tried to knee him in his crotch, but I couldn't. I kicked out at him, but without my arms I was powerless. I even tried to head butt him, but that didn't work on a guy like him. He laughed at me, and fuck... I saw two guys coming in by the long French windows leading out to the balcony. Holloway was moving with me toward them.

He didn't get far though, and neither did they.

Three shots sounded, rippling through the air one after the other.

Bang, bang... bang.

That was all I heard. The two guys dropped dead before me, the bullets going straight to their heads, and the grip Holloway had around my arms loosened.

"Holloway." I winced as he released me completely.

I snapped around to see his eyes roll back in his head before he fell. The bullet got him in his neck.

My eyes raised to meet Dad's, and I observed the vicious expression he had on his face and the strength he exuded with his two guns held out in front of him. He looked like a mobster, and not just any old mobster either. He looked like he would kill you with one look.

Another shot sounded.

It came from Luc. He shot Jefferson straight in his head.

Something … something strange happened in my heart as the seconds passed and it sunk in. Reality sunk in. The reality of what had just taken place.

Jefferson and Holloway. My friends, now dead, again because of me. These people after my father lured them over to darkness, relying on their greed, and now they were no more.

Jefferson and Holloway. I'd known them for the same length of time I knew Max and Sinclaire. So much had happened in so little time.

Unlike the normal energy I'd feel when we

defeated the bad guys, I felt sick. I looked back to Dad, and he lowered his guns, two Berettas.

"Amelia." He took a step toward me but stopped. A stream of blood ran down the line from his nose to the top of his lip, and he dropped the guns as he collapsed.

"Dad!" I rushed up to him. Luc joined us in panic.

"Boss, shit!" Luc lifted his head, but Dad looked so lifeless.

Tears ran down my cheeks at his lifeless form. "Dad, wake up."

I couldn't lose him too, not now. Not now.

One breath escaped his lips, and more blood poured from his nose. I pressed my hand to his neck searching for a pulse, but I couldn't feel one.

CHAPTER 2

Amelia

I sat next to Dad's bed, watching him.

He was sleeping now. The doctors had come to the house and said he'd overexerted himself, but really, what had happened was to be expected for someone in his condition.

He was fading fast. He put on a front, a very harsh exterior, and sometimes didn't look as sick as he was. He looked frail and not like the father I'd known ten years ago but still strong.

Even now as he lay in bed.

He'd come to for a few minutes earlier, and I

wanted to see him awake properly before I moved from his side. I couldn't bear it if I left him and he left me forever.

I didn't even get involved in the clearing away of those who'd died in our library. *Jefferson and Holloway.*

I tried not to think about them either. It made me sick that it was them. Better if it had been Roose who'd turned on me because I wasn't close to him. Not that I wished Roose dead. Never that. But I was having a hard time dealing with the truth.

Dad shuffled, moving his head, drawing my attention back to him.

His eyes fluttered open, and he looked at me. I grabbed a bottle of water and placed a straw in it, so he could sip and stay in the same position.

"Dad," I breathed.

There was a rasp in my voice, probably from not talking for hours. I hadn't seen Luc in about two hours. Not since the doctor left.

I held the water for Dad to sip. He took a small sip and a deep breath after, then reached for my hand.

"You look just like her when we first met," he told me, trying to smile but failing.

He was talking about Mom.

"People said I look more like you." I was trying for lighthearted but failing.

"When you were little, amore mio. Bella Amelia, my little girl."

I wish he wouldn't talk that way because it felt so reflective and final.

I pressed down hard on my lips to keep from crying, but it wasn't working.

How I hated to cry. I hated it because for me it was always about sadness. I'd never cried tears of joy. I'd never experienced that emotion people talk about when you are so overwhelmed with joy it makes you cry.

"Dad, please, you have to rest. You should have stayed away and not get involved. Luc and I could have handled those guys."

He gave my hand a gentle squeeze and arched his lip. "Luc, just Luc, not you. This is not you, and when a man sees his child in danger, he's not going to stand by and watch like a schmuck."

"Dad you're... sick."

"No, I'm past sick. I've gone past that stage, and I accept it. Right now, I'm only trying to be useful to you in whatever way I still can."

My eyes fell to the blue and gray square patterns on his bed sheets, then climbed up to meet his.

"I wish things could have been different." That he wasn't dying; like ten years hadn't gone by without us seeing each other.

"Me too, but that was for me to fix. There was never going to be any other ending for me, Amelia. I'm a bad person. You know that more than most. I've killed mindlessly. I shouldn't have killed Agent Peterson..." he stated with reflection.

Like always, I recalled that incident. Dad shooting Agent Peterson in his arms and legs, the men carrying him off through the door so Dad could finish him off. Although I'd never seen his end, I knew then how it would happen.

Dad would cut off his head, and he did. I remembered the news story. That was what had sent me through those doors ten years ago. It sent me through those doors with the mindset to leave forever.

This story, and any remorse he felt, was almost lost on me because it affected me deeply. I understood why he did it, but my soul couldn't accept it. I couldn't accept it.

"We... shouldn't talk about that now. We shouldn't. *You* shouldn't." I nodded.

"I don't want to die knowing you hate me." Sadness filled his eyes.

"I don't hate you. I never did, even when I told

you I did." Those were some of my last words I'd said to him before I left years ago. I'd told him I hated him, and then begged him to let me go. "I never hated you, and maybe I hated that I couldn't."

"I wish I had all those years back to make it up to you."

"Dad, don't, just... we can't live in regret. We both lost a lot, but we have now." That was me sounding a lot stronger than I really felt.

I squeezed his hand and continued to hold the tears back in.

The door opened, and Luc came in.

I couldn't help it; my body moved to him before I could even register what I did. I moved straight into his awaiting arms, where he held me and lulled me into the safe haven of him.

"Take her, take her and take care. I'm okay," Dad said.

Luc ran his hand over the top of my head and kissed my forehead.

Luc took me to my room, sat me down on the bed, and looked around the place first before joining me.

He took both my hands into his and looked straight into my eyes. I didn't think I'd ever seen Luc look so stern. Normally, there was an opening in the hardness he displayed. It was the place where I could reach him. Felt like it was just for me. Only for me.

"I love you," he told me. His voice was soft and soothing, unlike the hardness in his expression and the tenseness in his jaw.

"I love you." I would never get tired of telling him that, and I would relish the sound of him telling me too.

This time though...

This time felt different to when we said it before. Only the other night, my heart couldn't have felt more joy, and my soul soared through to the heavens at the declaration of this man's love.

This time when he said it, I felt that air of change again. The same change I'd felt before I found out who he really was.

Things were going to change again, and not for the good.

"I..." I didn't know what to say to him. There was so much to say, but where did I begin? With the stab of betrayal I felt knowing Jefferson and Holloway would have fed me to the lions for money? The sting, the poisonous sting of hurt that coursed through me as I listened to Jefferson tell me how this fucking plan rolled out?

Or should I talk about how I felt now, knowing they were both dead?

"I saw you dance today." He smiled and rubbed his thumb over the top of my hands, which looked so small in his.

This was so unlike what I thought we'd talk about, but this man knew me. He knew how to reach me.

"You did." I blinked several times, still trying to hold the tears back.

"You were amazing. You never cease to amaze me." He released my hand to brush the underside of my cheek. "I love you for that. I've never said those words to anyone. Just my mom, who never deserved to hear it."

I searched his eyes and felt the love he spoke of even more.

"Me neither. I've never said those words to anyone either, just my parents."

"No?" The hint of a smile that flickered across his face broke through to that place I could reach.

"Just you."

"So, I guess that's settled then. I'm more than the dog with mange."

Just like the first time when he joked about

that I felt bad at the comparison. He thought my feelings for him were comparable to what you'd feel if your dog had manage. You can't stand the sight of it but you love it enough to keep around.

I sucked in a breath and held on to it, still trying to hold the tears in. "You aren't like a dog with mange. I always knew how I felt about you, and it didn't matter who you were."

He cupped my face now with both hands. "Me for you too, Amelia. From the minute I first saw you. I love that you can switch into this angelic being of purity and everything amazing to create something so beautiful. But your strength is like nothing I've ever seen too."

"I don't feel strong, Luc." My lips trembled.

"You think you don't feel it, but it's there, deep inside you. Goddess, amore mio." He leaned in closer and pressed his head to mine, brushing his nose against mine.

Amore mio...

"Luc..." I said breathlessly.

"Goddess, I need you to do me a favor, please."

"Of course."

"I need you to be strong. I need you to be a cop, Taylor."

He'd never called me that, not even when I'd insisted after our first meeting. Taylor was the badass cop persona I'd created for myself all these long years. She was a ruthless, no-nonsense woman who was a warrior.

"*Taylor.*"

"Yes, remember our game... being whoever we want to be."

"I remember."

"You need to be her, just for a little longer. It will help you deal with the loss of your friends in whatever way you lost them. I... I killed Jefferson."

"You had to."

"I still killed him. Blood on my hands."

A tear ran down my cheek, and he caught it. "Luc, please, don't blame yourself."

"Let's focus on you. Amelia, there's someone here we can't trust, so until we find out who that is, don't trust anyone. Don't speak to anyone, at all. You understand me?" His jaw set and a wrinkle furrowed his brows.

"Yes." I couldn't begin to imagine who the person could be. I broke eye contact and started picking at the frays on the gold tassels of the pillow case.

"I mean it, Amelia. You have to suspect everyone."

I raised my gaze back to his. The hard look in

his blue gaze, lethal and stony displayed the wealth of his seriousness.

I knew he was right. It was just hard.

Who the hell could it be? It was only Dad and me who had known where the key would be.

We hadn't spoken to anyone about it. We'd sat in the garden talking after the meeting yesterday, and he gave me the key, along with the password for the diamonds at the facility in Rockford. It was just us, then...

Millicent came. Millicent had come with a tray of food...

Millicent...

No... She'd caught the end of our conversation. We were talking about doing something for the day.

Instantly, I felt terrible for even considering her. Millicent was like a mother to me, and a good friend to Dad.

"Luc, I don't know who it is." I shook my head.

"Someone knew exactly where you put the key, and they contacted the other guys. This is getting too far out of hand."

"Who could it be, Luc?"

"Anyone. I'm going to check the place out again to see if it's bugged, but I need you to be strong. I need you to be the badass cop I first met who would have handed my ass to me."

Again, I nodded. "I will try. What about you? I know you feel bad about Jefferson. You shouldn't feel bad."

"My dear Amelia, I am a mobster. That is who I'll be, and so I guess we're not playing games anymore."

I knew what he meant in saying that. He'd talked about changing; today showed me it wasn't that easy.

Not easy at all, and I couldn't blame him.

It was just that we were right back to square one. I was a cop, and he was a mobster. Like he said, the games were over. We could pretend to be whoever we wanted to be, but truth was truth.

CHAPTER 3

Luc

I waited until Amelia fell asleep, then I left her.

It was late but not late enough to turn in and not get shit done. The time to relax and watch the situation had long passed. Now, it was time to change things up.

Time to change.

Change everything and utilize my skills and abilities.

I'd grown soft. Over the last few months, I'd grown fucking soft and allowed the image and handle I had on things before I left for LA to slip out of my grasp.

I had to get that guy I used to be back. Now more than ever because now was when it mattered to me.

I was in love with her. I was obsessed with her.

Amelia, my goddess. Today, things could have gone way wrong.

Who is the rat? Who is the fucking rat?

Throughout the day, I'd gone through a list of people who'd been in the house with us since we'd been in Chicago. No one stood out to me.

I wasn't here all the time, so I didn't get to see all the people who came in and out.

Each time I'd been here, it was just me, Raphael, Amelia, and occasionally Millicent. Dad and Claudius had come by yesterday morning. That was it. All I knew of.

The part that was missing was, who was here when Amelia and Raphael were talking about the key and the safe in the library.

The place had to be bugged. Maybe the phone lines. Maybe they had some sort of device that would still let them listen in.

Based on that theory, the first thing I did was get one of my guys to check out the phone lines. I waited for confirmation of that being done before

I entered the meeting room, where the crew were all waiting for me.

They were all here, all the main guys who made up the core of the team, and a few others. The total was about twenty.

All hands on deck. Pa was here, as was part of my team, my boys Louis, Saul, and Donny. Missing from my team was my best friend, Maurice, but he had his own task of taking care of Gigi in LA with the rest of my team.

Claudius and his men were here too. We called them The Four.

Gio, Jude, Alex, and Dante. Like Claudius, they had a cross tattooed on either their necks or their cheeks in memory of their fallen ones. They operated as a separate unit. We trusted those guys the most, as they could shift from being bodyguards to mercenaries to assassins. My guys were good, but these guys were who you called when you needed to get shit done, like yesterday. Like Claudius, they killed without thinking about the consequences. Often because their targets were the worst kind. People like Victor who needed to be killed on sight.

I needed them to stay here with Raphael and Amelia.

All acknowledged me with respect as I walked

in. It felt like forever since I'd acted as my role as capo for the Rossi family. Claudius and I had the same title, but now I was boss. Or acting boss, *whatever*. This was the first time I'd stepped up in this way. We were both leaders but normally, for something like this, we'd have been sitting side by side, taking orders. Orders that would have come from Raphael. Our boss.

Everyone knew I'd been chosen to take the lead. I'd turned it down, but they didn't know that part yet. Claudius did though. Amelia had taken charge the other day, and I was proud of her for the way she'd handled Raphael, but things had changed big time. Things had changed, and she was in no state to do anything. Not like this. She didn't know our way. This was all above her. I needed her to be strong, not to take any form of lead in the business, but for herself.

I gazed to the far side of the room at Pa. Ever and always the arm of support as Raphael's consigliere, the trusted advisor. It was amazing. We all played our roles and did what we did best. We had to adapt to whatever was thrown our way and just know what to do. Pa, though, was consistent. He was consistent in his role always. Always the man you could trust with anything. Your secrets and your life.

"Thank you all for coming," I began.

I closed the door and stood in front of the large mahogany desk.

They all looked at me with anticipation. As I looked them over, I wondered what Amelia would think when she saw them. The sight of so many raw-blooded gangsters would probably freak her out.

"Needs must," Saul cooed in that eerie sing-song voice that gave even me the chills. He smiled, revealing a row of silver teeth, and the scar running across his face became more pronounced.

I nodded to him in respect, and he returned the gesture with a curt nod.

"Plans have changed." Only a few of them knew the original plan to go to the facility in Rockford to get the diamonds, but that was fine. They knew what I meant by saying plans had changed. It meant we had to up our game. It would be the only reason for a meeting like this in Raphael's house. "We need to hunt and bring down these guys on sight if you see them. Victor Pertrinkov and Tag. Those guys and anyone working for them. But we focus on them. Bring those two down, and the others will disappear like vermin. The plan is this: Claudius," I looked at my brother, who was staring at me with keen eyes. One bright blue like mine, the other a light brown. I could tell he was worried about me just from the look in them. The cross on his cheek inched higher when he pressed his lips together. "You and The Four stay here with Amelia and Raphael."

"Really? No disrespect, but you want the best guys to sit around like ducks and play babysitter?" Claudius quirked a brow at me.

"I need you to protect. Today, those guys got on the premises without being seen. We didn't have backup. There were four of them in the house, and a car drove away with God knows how many. They could have taken Amelia."

The CCTV and security system were disabled for protection. It was the first thing we'd insisted on when we got to Chicago, but that had been to our detriment. If Raphael hadn't made an old-fashioned trip wire, we would have had a very nasty surprise.

"I see." Claudius nodded.

He still didn't look like he'd accepted my answer, but he would never question me in front of the guys.

"Marcus." I always addressed my father by his name when we were in company like this. "I need you with Raphael."

He gave me a simple nod, but the pride that

beamed from him as he watched me was evident. He'd probably waited his whole life to see me stand here taking the lead. Me or Claudius. Probably more for me though. I hadn't told him yet that I was going to disappoint him when I stepped down and took on the clean way of life if I got the chance. If I got the chance, I would go wherever Amelia and I could be happy.

"As for me and my crew, we'll search for Tag and Victor, hunt them down. Saul, you're with me, but I need you to call in a favor from the Galluccios." This was the power we had. The power I had. The other crime families and the Rossis lived together in a symbiotic relationship and cooperated to keep things that way. There were some guys we couldn't touch because if we did, it meant instant war, others who wanted in on our turf. The thing was, Raphael practically owned Chicago, and they would have a hard time getting anywhere near us to try anything stupid. "Donny and Louis, link up with the capos for the Romanos and the Bellefontes and scour the east and west sides."

Donny and Louis looked pleased with that. They got on well with those guys.

"Please tell me we get free reign of what we can do," Donny stated, eyeing me with his sharp eyes. He reminded me of a fox; cunning like one too.

"The orders are this: If you see anyone who shouldn't be here, kill them." I looked at Claudius and The Four as I said that. Then I looked to my boys. Saul, Donny, then Louis. "If you see Tag or Victor, kill them. Gather intel from any lackeys you find, then kill them. Don't give them a chance to get away and regroup. Men, we have to step this game up and do this. Blood for blood. We jump out there on the battlefield and take these fucktards out. This shit has taken far too long already." That was Raphael's fault. The man should have just gotten a crew together like I am now to hunt Tag and Victor, but then… I wouldn't have known Amelia, would never have had the chance to fall for her. No way was I going to let anything get to her. "Blood for fucking blood."

This was it.

It was time for war.

"Blood for blood," they all chanted in unison.

"Meeting adjourned. We meet back here as soon as we can regroup. Hopefully with their heads."

"I like heads." Saul laughed, whipping out a long reach knife.

"As do I," Donny agreed, tipping the brim of his fender.

Louis remained silent as always, but I knew he

was in. They were the first to leave, then Saul. I walked out, leaving Claudius, Dad, and The Four, but I knew Claudius would follow me.

It was almost predictable.

We walked into Raphael's office, and he closed the door.

"You looked good out there, little brother. Sure you really don't want to be boss?" Claudius smiled wide and raised his brows.

I sat on the edge of Raphael's desk and frowned. "You know how I feel."

"Yup, it's kind of clear. How are you holding up?"

I smirked. It was funny how he knew to ask me that. He knew me, and it was times like this when I valued the relationship we had.

"I don't know how to answer that. I'm not okay, if that's what you mean. There's a fucking rat in the house, and things could have gone south today. They got on the premises without being seen."

"It wasn't that they got on the premises without being seen. They just knew when to come," Claudius pointed out, pulling up a chair and sitting down in front of me.

"Fuck, who the fuck is it? It must be the phones or something."

Claudius shook his head. "No, we had the associate from the CIA look into it earlier. Luc, there's no trace of anything like that. He said there's always something normally undetectable to the standard equipment the police and the feds use but not the CIA. They found nothing. So..."

"It was actually someone who was here." My heart sank at the thought. "I need you to question the house staff."

"Already ahead of you, brother." He straightened and focused more keenly on me. "The butler and the housekeeper."

God, I didn't want to venture down that path, and that was why I was leaving Claudius here. He had the balls it took to take you down if needed. No questions, no in-between, no gray area. It was what it was. A traitor was a traitor.

"The butler and the housekeeper." I repeated.

"If its them, they're dead."

I didn't know the butler all that well, but Millicent was... she'd been part of the family forever. She'd told me yesterday that she'd looked after Amelia since birth. She was the next best thing to my father in the chain of command. Kept Amelia secret, too, from all of us. The same way Dad had. All those long years of serving Raphael, and neither had let on to anyone that Amelia even existed.

It couldn't be Millicent. I really didn't think it was.

"Yes, I get it."

"Do you? Because you look like you don't." Claudius narrowed his eyes.

"I get it," I said with more emphasis.

"Whoever it is started this war, Lucian. We lost a lot of men because of greed and selfishness. Whoever it is, is dead to me. No chances, no excuses. I just wish I were joining you on the battlefield."

"I need you here because I can't be here. I need to be actively doing something. Looking for Victor, looking for Tag. There's no one else I trust more than you."

"Means a lot." He tipped his head in reverence and his long hair swayed about his shoulders. "What about the diamonds? I'm not sure if you should abandon the plan to get them. You didn't mention it, so I'm assuming they're at the bottom of the list."

"I think we need to up the game and take down Tag and Victor. Take away the elements, which are the things they want, and hit them hard." It was a good plan because if we were successful, it would eliminate the threat. Simple. "It got dangerous when they were able to just come here, walk onto the grounds like they were walking in the park. It's fucked up. We need to focus."

"Alright, watch your back, Lucian." He cocked his head to the side and drew in a deep breath.

Watch my back? Sure, I wished it was just my back I had to worry about. My mouth felt dry and my throat constricted. It was time to get serious.

Time to go. I wanted a head start.

I sighed and moved toward the door.

"Lucian, you need to rest." His words stopped me.

I turned back to face him. "I can't. I can't rest."

"You need to. You need to go rest and be with your woman for tonight. I'll go out and patrol the old district and be back in the morning, then you can take over."

"Claudius, I—"

"No," he cut me off and rose to stand. "No. You're boss, but I'm your older brother."

I chuckled. "You know if I wanted to go, you couldn't stop me?"

"I could, but you wouldn't like the way I did it." He grinned.

I sighed. I guess I was exhausted, and being with Amelia was good for me right now.

"Shoot my legs off?"

"Something like that. At least your girl will love you no matter if you have legs or not." He came closer and rested a hand on my shoulder. "Go, be with her. Tomorrow, I'll make sure the boys and I guard her with our lives."

"Thank you."

"No thanks needed. Boss."

I was reminded of how annoyed he'd been when Raphael chose me and not him. He moved past me and went through the door.

I then headed back upstairs to Amelia's room.

I expected her to be sleeping, but she was sitting up on the bed wide awake.

CHAPTER 4

Luc

"I thought you were sleeping," I moved to sit next to her on the bed.

Amelia hugged her knees to her chest. The motion caused the delicate straps of her negligee to slip down her shoulders.

"I was," she replied, voice faint and weary. "I just woke up and couldn't go back to sleep. There were voices in the house, strange people… just like before."

"Before?" I didn't know what she meant.

"The night my mother died. My father's men

came here. It was the first time I saw what we were... Not normal." She looked troubled.

"Amelia—" She stopped me with a kiss. She moved so quickly to my lips that I didn't even register what she was doing.

I was about to launch into my strength pep talk from earlier, but the kiss robbed me of my thoughts.

She moved and shuffled so that she was in my lap, then those long golden legs wrapped around me as she straddled me.

I kissed her back with the same passion she fed me, indulging in her hot, wet mouth, indulging in the taste of her.

Indulging in her and all that made this woman mine.

"Luc, make love to me." Her whisper was like a feather-soft caress on my lips. "I want it like how it was before, when we were just wild and free and indulged in each other."

"Here?" I was very aware that this was her bedroom and Raphael was nearby. "You sure we won't give your father a heart attack?" I didn't know where the strength came from to chuckle, but I did.

She moved back and gave me a sassy look that oozed seduction. When she reached for the hem of that already sexy-as-hell negligee and pulled the thing over her head to unveil her beautiful naked body, my heart stilled and my cock instantly hardened.

The vision of her sexiness was enhanced when she loosened the band holding her hair up in a ponytail and that gorgeous mass of hair tumbled down her shoulders and over her fully rounded breasts. My eyes zeroed in on her taut strawberry-pink nipples begging to be sucked.

"You can touch me if you want to Lucian. I swear my dad won't come in here. His room's several doors down." She smiled as I continued to stare. "You're looking at me like it's the first time you've seen me naked."

"It's always like the first time, and yes, I will touch you." I absolutely fucking would. "Lie down and open your legs. I want to make you feel good. Make you forget everything."

She did as I asked, resting back against the stack of pillows and opening her legs.

She was a beautiful, sexy sight and all mine for the taking. The pretty little pink thong she wore just enhanced the vision of her.

Her wearing nothing but that, hair sprawled out around her and that golden skin stark against the pink lace.

I backed off my jacket and took hold of her tiny waist as I moved onto the bed. In that instant, I got sucked into the temptation of her, and I was the one who forgot everything. Damn, I forgot it all. Where we were, who we were, what we were.

I was just Luc, the man who wanted her to be mine, and I hoped like hell she just felt like Amelia. My goddess.

I lowered my head to take her right nipple into my mouth, and she arched into me, throwing her head back as she pressed the ample flesh of her breast against my face. Her desperate moan of ecstasy made me suck harder and take more of her breast into my mouth. As much as I could get so that I could please her.

"Luc..." came her jagged breath. I had to look up at her and smile, loving the sight of what I did to her unfold itself on me.

I moved to the neglected breast and took the desperate nipple in when she inched her head back up to gaze at me.

She watched me as I sucked and ran her hand through my hair, encouraging me to stay.

I stayed for as long as I could, ravishing the delicacy of her beauty. I would have stayed forever, but that would mean me finishing in my pants just from listening to the moans of pleasure that slipped from between her lips.

I pulled back and trailed kisses all along the valley of her delicious mounds, down to the delicate dragonfly and butterfly tattoo on her left hip, across the flat of her toned stomach, and down to the fine bone structure of her pelvis.

With a wicked smile, I moved the lace fabric of her panties away and turned my smile up a notch when I saw the sweet honey nectar from her pretty pussy. She was wet and ready for me.

But I wouldn't take her yet. Not yet.

She gasped when I tore away the thong, ripping it off her. I didn't want to spare the seconds it would take to slide them down her legs. I wanted them gone now. Then I dove straight in, face buried between her thighs. She writhed beneath the firm grasp I had on her hips when I pushed my tongue into her pussy. Licking and sucking, I teased the hard nub of her clit and drank the sweet nectar that flowed from her, desperate for more. And more.

Her thighs tensed, and her moans became more labored. I reached up for her breasts and was satisfied when I felt how hard her nipples were. It meant she was close to orgasm. The second confirmation I could see when I glanced down at her feet was her pretty little pink toes curling into the satin sheets.

"I'm coming, Luc," she hummed.

"Not yet, goddess." That was new. I'd never said that to her before.

A bewildered look crossed her face. "Ughhh... ahhhhh. Luc, I have to."

"Hold it. Come when I say." With another smile, I stroked her in long, teasing strokes and relished in the desperation that brimmed in her beautiful eyes.

"Please, I have to."

"No, amore mio, you never have to beg me. Just trust me when I say you'll enjoy it more this way."

She sucked in a breath and held on to my shoulder, squeezing down hard with her fingers pressing into my skin through the cotton of my shirt.

Lowering my head again, I continued to incite the pleasure I wanted to give her. My tongue once again pushed into her core, but instead of the wildness I'd first exhibited, I licked her in short, precise strokes. That made her squirm, like I'd hoped, and when I had her right where I wanted her, I moved away and placed two fingers inside her, moving in and out the same way I would with my cock.

The shocked look on her face turned me on even more. Before she could get over that, I moved back to her breast and sucked hard. Fucking her with my fingers and tasting her delicious breasts, both of them, alternating from one to the other. It was fucking amazing.

When I felt like she couldn't handle any more, I decided to release her from the pleasure-filled torture.

I moved up to her lips and brushed my mouth over hers. "Come for me, goddess."

Her eyes that had been squeezed tight flew open, and she sucked in a deep sharp breath but released it on a ragged breath and moaned into her glorious orgasm.

"Luc…" she cried out, and I was so glad that Raphael was a few doors down. I seriously hoped he didn't hear that. Maybe he did. Maybe the others did too, but fuck it. I didn't care.

What I cared about was having her in this moment of raw passion and succumbing to the will and hold it had on us. Whoever the fuck heard wouldn't be dumb enough to come in here and disturb us, Raphael included. He'd wanted me to win his daughter's heart, and I had. I had and lost my heart to her too.

I lost my heart and my soul to her.

"Good girl." My fingers were soaked with her heavenly juices, which I moved up to my mouth to taste, then I leaned back down to her core so I could drink the rest.

Her skin felt hot, and I was almost buzzing with the energy I sensed from her.

Light fingers fluttered over my face, and I returned my gaze to hers to see her smiling.

"You're the devil," she cooed.

"Yes... I am." I meant that in more ways than one. I was the devil for her, the devil that turned her to my dark world of crime and blood for blood.

But she was the queen of my heart and soul. I bent only to her will.

"I'm not done with you yet," I reminded her.

"Take me," she cooed on a wild breath and with lust in her eyes.

"I plan to." I shrugged out of my clothes and tossed them to the corner of the room, then I flipped her over, so that she was on her hands and knees with her beautiful, firm ass pushed out for me to take.

Her hair fell forward over her angelic face, turning up the sexiness of her. Unable to tamp down my need to be inside her, I guided my cock to her entrance and thrust right inside. Her knees wobbled from the impact, and the tightness of her pretty pussy almost made me come right there. Just from that one thrust.

She moaned out loud again, and I caught sight of us in the corner of her long standing mirrors. The sight was purely erotic and hot with her massive tits bobbling in front of her as I started a slow pump, then sped up. I grabbed her hips and increased my pace before I held it, staying in that rhythm we both loved.

Fire licked at my skin in wild, hot flames of desire and passion. Her skin felt hot to touch too, just like before but hotter. She was already moaning loud, but my increased pace and pounding made her cry out even more.

When I started rutting into her like an animal, we both started moaning.

That was when I verged on the precipice of my own release.

"Amelia, I'm going to fuck you hard." Hard just the way she liked it.

Fucking hell, this time felt different to any other time. Make love, have sex, fuck. This was everything and something else on its own.

She winced and moaned, grasping for the sheets and panting.

Passion seized me and took control of my body,

taking her too. We couldn't stop it. I couldn't stop it, and I didn't want to. My release exploded from me on a hot, virile eruption. Filling me with the flames of fire that licked over my skin.

She came again too, and the walls of her core grabbed me tight, milking me dry, draining me inside her.

We both collapsed in a hot sexual heap, breathing hard from the wildness of our love making.

I pulled her against my chest, holding her tight, holding her to me where I wanted to keep her forever.

I wished I could.

I had her two more times before we fell asleep. Drunk on love. I held her in my arms, and we stayed that way.

When morning broke, reality came with it, and I knew I had to leave. I just didn't want to yet.

Not yet.

Not... yet.

She didn't even know the plan, and I didn't want to tell her yet.

Those feather-soft fingers fluttered over my

forearm, rubbing along the edge where fine hairs covered the surface of my skin. She lingered on the Japanese character for *earth* I had tattooed on the crook of my elbow.

"Morning," she cooed, twisting around to face me.

I moved down to kiss her and rubbed my finger over her breast to play with her right nipple.

"Morning, baby. Did you have a nice sleep?"

"I did. I dreamt we were in Italy, at the villa."

I smiled at the thought. Yes. What a good thought. I'd always talked about that villa, and in one of my dreams, she lay naked in the sea of gardenias in the front garden. She lay there under the moonlight in all her glory and beauty.

"Were you naked in the garden of gardenia's?" I chuckled.

"No, but they were there. I was sitting in the grass watching you."

"What was I doing?" I loved the radiance of the sun washing over her, picking out the lighter brown parts of her eyes.

"Walking toward me with a bonsai tree. Butterflies surrounded you. Pink ones like the ones that live in Italy."

I cupped her face, feeling my heart swell. "It will happen."

When we first met, I'd introduced her to my love of flowers and gardening. I had a bonsai tree I'd had for years. I was dumb when I took it to LA and stupid to surround the thing with butterflies. That whole setup must have withered away by now. I hadn't seen my plant in over a month.

It was so stupid to think of such a thing now. Maybe I'd be lucky enough to make it through all this craziness and become the gardener, and she the dancer.

It seemed like a dream because if I knew anything, it was that this was another quiet before the storm. The last few weeks were part of the game. Part of Victor's game.

I didn't know Tag, but I knew enough from what I'd seen over the last few weeks to know he was probably crazier than Victor.

"I wished I'd known you when I was last here." Her voice broke into my thoughts.

I chuckled at that. "Amelia, in case you didn't notice, I'm five years older than you. Your father would have killed me himself if he'd caught me sniffing around you. You were seventeen."

"So?"

"I would have been twenty-two and asking for my ass to end up dead or in prison."

"Would that stop you?" A sexy smile filled her face because she knew my answer.

"No."

"We could have seen each other in secret. I was a few weeks away from my eighteenth birthday when I left."

She was a few weeks away from her birthday again.

"I would have been your first. I would have made love to you for your birthday."

"I wish," she breathed.

She held my gaze, and we both seemed to know that while this talk was nice, we'd have to get up and break out of this bubble of passion we'd created.

"Amelia..." I smoothed my hands under her chin.

"I know... you have to go... or something. I don't know what's going on, but I can see in your eyes that you're leaving."

"Claudius will stay here with his men."

"Why can't you stay?" She frowned and a grimace pulled at the corners of her delicate mouth.

"I need to search. I need to do something. I know how Victor works, and I have a few hunches about where I may find intel on him. Claudius will take care of you. You and Raphael."

"I want you." She squeezed her eyes shut, then opened them again.

"I can't stay here and let what happened yesterday happen again. I can't." My stomach tensed.

"What if something bad happens to you?" Pain darkened her eyes and she tucked her hair behind her ear.

I rubbed my temples and thought of how I could choose my next words carefully. Something bad could most assuredly happen to me, and there was the other reason why I thought Claudius was the better person to stay with her.

She sat up and quickly pulled the sheet to her chest, shoulders tensed and mouth rigid. "That's why..."

No way could she have sensed my fears.

I sat up too. "Why what?"

"You think something bad could happen to you, so that's why you want Claudius to take care of me." There was a rise in her tone as she spoke and she gave me an incredulous stare.

Fuck, seems like she was right there inside my head. "Amelia, you don't know Victor like I do. If he comes here with God knows who to take you,

Claudius is the only person I know who can stop that from happening."

"It's like you're just giving up." Now her stare became distant – empty – and her chin trembled.

"I'm not. I just can't allow anything bad to happen to you. Not like Henry."

The minute I said Henry's name, she stopped mid-breath of her next words. Henry had been my best friend. Him and Maurice, we were it. Claudius was always there for me, and he was a brother in every sense. But those guys were like family too. Victor took Henry, his wife, their kids; Jack and my sweet goddaughter, Susanna, and killed them. He'd created a sick game no one would ever win and fucked with our emotions.

Fucked with my emotions. I'd thought I'd saved those kids, but I'd watched them draw their last breath as the poison Victor had fed them robbed them of life.

I would never forget it as long as I lived. I only dealt with it because I thought I'd exacted vengeance when I was of the mistaken belief that I'd killed Victor.

But the fucker came right back from the dead. That was five years ago. As to where that bastard had been all this time, I didn't know. He'd just emerged when this war began. That again signaled the kind of power Tag had.

I didn't want to admit this, but it was above me. And I was tainted because I was thinking with my heart.

"Luc." She winced.

"No, don't argue with me, Amelia. I'm leaving, and you're staying here, where capable people can take care of you."

I didn't want to spoil what we had last night and all that we'd shared.

"I'm not helpless. I'm not this helpless person you make me out to be."

I slid off the bed and reached for my pants and boxers. "Amelia, these aren't the guys you're used to in LA These people aren't like Jefferson or Holloway. You aren't helpless, but this is above you."

That was it all I had left to say. She frowned at me in a huff, but she would have to be upset with me because this was the best way.

Better for us both.

CHAPTER 5

Amelia

I wanted to be furious. I wanted to feel angry at Luc for his decision, but in my heart, I knew he was doing what he thought was best for me.

He was making some sort of sacrifice that he felt would benefit me in some way. It didn't help, though, that the man I loved had basically left me in what he deemed to be capable hands and thrown himself out to the lions to hunt the people who were hunting us.

He'd left about two hours ago. I went to check on Dad first and found he was still asleep. Then I went downstairs to get the shock of my life when I saw who was waiting for me. It felt like I'd just walked onto the set of something like *The Terminator*.

Claudius and four guys who looked just as hard and vicious as him practically guarded the premises.

Two at the front entrance, two at the back, and I was told the other entrances were sealed off. The guys all had crosses tattooed on their cheeks or their necks. Claudius had a cross on his cheek. It seemed to mean something now that I saw them all together. More than just a cool tattoo.

I knew they were all here to protect me, but damn, it reminded me of before. Just like I had been reminded last night. Strange men in the house. Tough guys, but these guys looked tougher. Like ex- military with the huge muscles and badass attitude.

The butler, whose name I couldn't remember, was questioned before entry, and the tallest guy was now questioning Millicent.

She looked petrified, and her dainty features looked smaller against the guy.

They were standing at the front door entrance.

"How long will you be on the premises?" The

guy asked her. His tone was rough. It added to the hardness in his composure.

"I planned to be here all day." Millicent answered. "Mr. Rossi has a special diet. After yesterday, I have to make sure he gets the proper nutrition."

"Give me your bag and spread your arms out," the guy ordered.

That was where I needed to step in.

"Hey, give her a break." I walked up to them and squared my shoulders off with him.

I must have looked comical because I was just a little taller than Millicent.

The guy laughed and regarded me with observant eyes. "Mrs. Boss, this is how things have to be."

"She doesn't need to spread her arms and be treated like some criminal. I know her."

"Right, word has it that you knew the other two guys from yesterday too. Word also has it that they wouldn't hesitate to kill you." He smirked, and the dimple in his left cheek softened his harshness and focused the attention on his sculpted looks.

"That was different, Mr...?"

"The names Dante, and no, Mrs. Boss, it wasn't different." The trace of amusement left his eyes. "If you want her in the house, she needs to do as I say. Now."

Oh my God, what the hell? This was my house. Well...

It was Dad's house.

"It's okay. I have nothing to hide," Millicent offered. She held out her bag and gave it to Dante.

He searched through it and motioned his head for her to spread her arms. She did, and I had to endure the embarrassment of him doing a scan of her and the whole search procedure of patting down the length of her to see if she was carrying a gun.

Millicent, of all the people. She was like Aunt May from Spiderman. And like a woman of that caliber who was in her late sixties, she looked embarrassed too.

"All clear, Mrs. Boss." He looked at me again.

"Why are you calling me that?" I challenged.

He laughed. "Aren't you?"

I linked my arm with Millicent's and ushered her away. We stopped in the kitchen, and I would have started talking to her, but Claudius came out of the pantry carrying a dead squirrel. I shrieked when I saw it.

"What the fuck are you doing in here with that?" I winced.

"Language, Miss Amelia," Millicent scolded. "Your mother would be appalled to hear you sound like some fish wife."

"Yes, I'd bet she fucking well would. This dead fucker might too," Claudius cooed, smiling and waving the squirrel's tail at Millicent.

She frowned and walked away from us.

"That is disgusting." I folded my arms under my breasts.

"It's protein. I don't know what the fuck kind of diet Raphe is on, but there's no meat in the house."

I shook my head at him. "You killed a squirrel?" I couldn't believe it. Nausea pulled at my stomach and I had to focus on not heaving.

"Man has to eat." He winked at me and placed the squirrel on the counter.

My skin tightened and burned, and it was difficult to swallow.

Suddenly it was all too much and I had the compulsion to flee, to be somewhere else. Somewhere that wasn't here.

"I'm going for a walk."

"Yeah, right, you're not."

More orders.

"I need air and space. I need to clear my head." I couldn't focus or concentrate in here. It really was too much and I was on the verge of tears. I hated crying and I would rather do it in private if tears were going to take me. It was this whole sense of helplessness. Being powerless in this situation and having to do as I was told.

"You need to stay inside the house and open a window if you need fresh air. Like fuck are you going wondering around for a damn walk."

"I just want to go outside," I argued.

"Amelia." He held a finger up at me and walked closer. His hair swished about his shoulders as he leaned in and got real close in my personal space.

He looked so much like Luc. I wished he didn't because I wanted Luc to be here right now, and he wasn't.

"What?"

"Stop acting like a fucking brat and get with the program. We're here guarding the house, and the reason why we are here is because we're the best at what we do. Right now, my brother is on the streets looking for these motherfuckers who want you dead, and I don't have his back. I always have his back. So no, you will not go for a walk or whatever the fuck it is you want to do. Capisce?"

First, I felt numb from the way he spoke to me. Then I felt awful about what he'd said. I was acting like a brat. It was because I was completely off my game and out of my element here.

"I got it." My shoulders slumped and I swallowed hard past the lump that had formed in my throat.

He backed away and held up a hand to his cheek where he'd had the cross tattooed.

"I'm sorry." I couldn't keep the quiver out of my voice. I failed at staving off the tremble in my shoulders too.

He stopped by the counter and looked at me. "What for?"

"This. I should be out there looking for them myself." I would go if they let me.

"That's not the way this works." His voice sounded strained. "I know Miss Badass Cop Amelia Rossi could go out there on a hunt too, but this is out of your league. You're a cop. They do things differently. Also, just because you're a cop doesn't mean you suddenly got what it takes to bring down fucking psychos."

He was right. I knew that, but it didn't make me feel any better. "It's just hard to stand by and wait while the man I love is out there and something could happen to him."

Against my will, a tear ran down my cheek. I quickly wiped it away and tried to shake off that heaviness that washed over my whole body. My heart shrinked away, backing into that cave of despair as worry tugged at my soul.

Luc... what is something happened to him? What would I do?

"Don't you dare cry. I don't know what the hell to do with a crying woman, and you don't look like the crying-type princess. I was assured there would be no tears."

I smirked and tried to hold the tears back, but they came.

"Fuck." He winced and reached for me, pulling me in for a hug. "I have squirrel hands."

"I actually don't care." I rested my head on his chest and allowed the tears to fall. The thing was, I wasn't the crying type of woman, and this wasn't me. He pulled back and took my hand, then led me out to the corridor. "Where are we going?"

"For a walk." He glanced down at me and smiled.

We walked outside, and he released my hand once we got on the path that led to the moors. I used to play out there as a child.

I wanted to walk around the gardens again and enjoy the flowers.

We got close to the entrance, but just as I was about to continue, he pulled me back.

"Here's good princess. Never can tell who might be lurking." His eyes darted about looking around with suspicion.

I gazed up at him. "Okay, thank you for this."

"It's fine. So... you love my brother?"

"Yes."

He looked uncomfortable and shifted his weight from one leg to the next.

"Well, it worked out well, then, and Raphe made a good choice."

"Choice? Was there someone else?" I hadn't thought of that.

He laughed. "Yeah, there kind of was. Me."

I searched his eyes, and the fascination of his eye color drew me in. One blue, the other brown. "You?"

He rocked back on his heels, and the back of his jacket whipped out in the wind as the breeze rustled between us.

"Yeah, me. You wouldn't have liked me, and you don't seem to like squirrels." He shook his head and smiled again.

I laughed. I couldn't believe I laughed. "It's gross, Claudius."

"Needs must. Anyway, I can see it. You and Lucian, you suit each other. I don't know about the whole cop thing though, but that's for you to work out."

That was another thing that was shelved to the back of my mind. There was a lot I had to face, and God, I needed to call Sinclaire and tell him about Jefferson and Holloway. I needed to tell him, even if he already knew. I'd spoken to Gigi briefly this morning. Brief because she was with Maurice and they'd sounded like the last time. like I'd interrupted something steamy. As long as they were safe, I was happy.

"I can't go back to that life."

"So, you want this?" He quirked a brow.

"This isn't me either."

"Hmmm, it's not Luc either. That's why I'm here and he's out there. That's why Raphael choose him and not me. He's a real hardass, ruthless in every sense of the word, and he'd make a good leader of a business like this, but he's different. He always was. We have to—" His voice trailed off as he looked ahead of me.

I turned to see what he was looking at, and my eyes bulged when I saw who it was that stood outside the fence to the premises.

Victor.

Victor Pertrinkov.

I could see the devilish smile on his face from

here. We were about twenty meters apart, but I could see it, and it made my skin crawl and chills race down my spine.

"Amelia, get inside." Claudius took hold of me.

Luc

"Did you get him?" I asked, gripping the phone as I pressed it to my ear.

That fucking Victor was outside the house. Jesus Christ. It was a joke. I was out here looking for him, and he was there. Right there with Amelia.

"No, we didn't get him," Claudius answered. "I sent Dante after him, and he came back empty. It was too late by the time we got back inside, and I didn't want to leave Amelia, just in case."

"You did right." I sighed. "We need to find out where they're staying."

"Intel got eyes on him that led out to the main road. We lost him after that."

"Could have gone anywhere. That route diverts to anywhere." Shit. This was complete shit.

I'd searched the old district with Saul and Giorgio, one of the Galioni guys. We'd come up with nothing.

I was sitting in a bar downtown now, regrouping. It was nearly midday. The bars were just opening, and this was one I used to come to all the time.

"I'll keep looking and let you know if we come up with anything."

"Thanks."

"And don't worry. We'll stay here as a unit. I don't know if today was a scare tactic, or if he was trying to lure us out."

"It's part of the game." He was there to remind us that we couldn't catch him. Asshole.

"Great, well, you know him more than I do."

"I'll talk to you later, Claudius."

"Speak later." He hung up.

I didn't have a chance to catch my breath before someone ran soft fingers over the back of my neck.

"Well, look who it is. My boy's returned."

I turned to see Maria. I guess I could have called her my on-again, off-again ex-girlfriend who'd been with me for the last couple of years.

I straightened on the stool and twisted, so I was facing her.

"Hey, how've you been?" My pulse quickened. It felt weird being in her presence.

"Really?" She raised her brows and gazed at me through her bright blue eyes. She had a slight tan, and it made her white blond hair look more striking. She was beautiful and the kind of woman I'd basically used because I knew she would always be available to me.

"Yes, really."

"Good, I suppose. You haven't called me in a while. I heard you found someone new."

God, I wasn't in the mood for this, but I kind of felt the time would creep up on me.

"Maria, look..."

She held up both hands and shook her head. "It's okay. We weren't exactly anything, even if I thought we were."

Maybe it was the fact that I'd had to tame my wildness for Amelia, but as I looked at the woman before me who I'd treated like nothing, I truly, truly felt like a complete bastard. A son of a bitch, literally, who'd acted like an asshole to her.

"I'm sorry. You deserve better."

She laughed. "That's a good one, but look at me. I'm the girl men use. You know first-hand, right? I bounce from one job to another, not really knowing what I'm doing with myself. It's cool though. One day, I'll know."

"Maria, you don't have to live like that."

"Well, it comes in handy sometimes. Come here." She smiled and crooked her finger. I leaned closer hoping like hell she wasn't going to kiss me because I didn't want to hurt her feelings any more than I had.

She slipped her arms around my neck and nuzzled her face against mine.

"Maria, I am with someone else, and—"

"Relax, lover boy. I'm helping you. Put your arm around me."

I did as she said wondering what she was going to do.

She cupped my face and brushed her nose against mine.

"There's a man sitting across the bar on the left. He came into Gullimi's last night. Your name was dropped a few times. He's watching us now," she whispered.

Fuck. "What does he look like?"

"Thin, longish hair, and a mole on his chin." Her eyes flicked up past mine then back to focus on me.

"What's he doing now?"

"Still watching. Another guy just joined him. They were both together last night."

"Hey, I don't want you hanging around bars like that. It's dangerous."

"You almost sound like you care." She giggled, running her fingers over my cheek.

I wondered how the fuck we must have looked to everyone else here.

Amelia would not be happy if she saw me like this.

"I do care. If you need money, you let me know."

"I don't need or want anything from you." She went to move away, but I pulled her back and bent low to her ear.

"I don't care if you want it or not, and I'm being serious." From inside my jacket, I took my wallet and gave it to her. I took her hand and closed her fingers around the hard leather. There were five hundred dollars cash in there and about ten grand on the credit card. "Get gone for a while. Use the cash first. It's enough to get out of Chicago and stay some place safe. Password for my credit card is 0100. Take everything on there."

"Luc—"

"Maria, I'm serious. You glued up to me like this just made you a target."

"I know." She held my gaze. "He, um... he took out his phone the minute I walked up to you. Maybe he's talking about you, maybe he's talking about me. Or both. Risky. But you take risks when you love someone." Her voice quivered.

My lips parted, and all I could do was stare. She loved me. I felt even worse now because I couldn't return the sentiment.

I'd known Maria for years. It had started wild and always stayed wild. It was just sex, nothing more, not even a date. She usually worked at the diner Claudius and I liked going to. When she saw me, she knew what I wanted. I should at least have some level of feelings for her to consider her mine at one point or another. But no. Not even now. Yet there was Amelia, who I'd only known for months.

"Maria, I..." There was nothing I could say that wouldn't make me sound like a jerk.

"I didn't say it for you to tell me back." A little smile tugged at the corners of her delicate mouth. "You'd be lying, and you've never been a liar."

"I care about you." I had to say something, and that was the truth.

She leaned in again and brushed her lips against my cheek. "Be careful, Lucian, and thanks."

She stepped back, still holding my gaze, then moved away from me.

I watched her until she left the bar, going through the large oak doors. The hair stood up on the back of my neck as I now felt like I was being watched.

Please be okay, Maria.

Later, I'd send someone to check on her. Right now, I had to take care of these guys.

I stood up and walked out back to where the dumpsters were. I hid in the alley way behind the metal door.

Just as I predicted, a man came through matching the description of what Maria had given me. As I'd walked out of the bar, I didn't need to look at him to get a picture. Doing it this way was enough. He stepped out and looked around with confusion on his stupid face.

The stupid look was the first to go when I slammed the door shut and jumped out at him. The fool tried to draw his gun, but he was too late. The fucker didn't get a chance to because I drew mine first and shot off his middle and forefinger. He screamed, and blood spurted from his hand.

His scream intensified when I headbutted him into the wall and grabbed his neck. I couldn't believe they'd sent this guy after me. Fucking pathetic. At least give me a challenge. Not this pansy ass Nancy boy.

"Where is Victor staying?" I barked, pressing his head into the wall.

"Let go of me, man," he wailed.

I pressed the barrel to my gun under his neck, and the man's eyes widened. "Talk the fuck now before I blow your brains out."

"More will come. Doesn't matter if you kill me," he taunted.

"Yes, I gathered as fucking much. But why waste one stupid asshole and time when I can torture the info from you?" There was a shuffling sound on the other side of the door. Maria had said there was another guy.

The door flung open, and out he came guns blazing. This guy was bigger, more in my league but not enough to take me down. I was a good shot, always. A bullet smacked right between his eyes before he could really get going.

I barely had to move the gun away from my new friend's neck.

The other guy crumpled to the ground, leaving his shocked friend.

"You didn't know who you were dealing with, did you?" I taunted, widening my eyes at him so he could see my wrath.

I got the shock of my life when the fool started laughing, then I noticed it. The red nose and the raw skin inside his nostrils. Then slightly dilated pupils that seemed to look more spaced out as I looked at him. He was a user. Some kind a drug addict.

Back in LA, Victor had killed Cole, Amelia's confidant in the underground. After his death, there was a guy called Brandon, a drug addict, snooping around, sniffing around like a fucking rat. A pawn. Definitely not a foot solider, just someone they'd sent to fuck with us. He'd ended up dead too.

This guy... he was one of them. He was a pawn, as was the other. People knew me, and these types of guys didn't approach a guy like me and expect to live. Victor knew that too.

And there wouldn't have been just two of them. Two runts of the litter that barely added up to one.

Fuck.

So, they were here for something else, then. What was it?

"Why are you following me?" I tightened my grip on him.

"To give you a message, mafia boss." He laughed, and his eyes did that crazy like jangle as he scrunched up his nose.

"Give me the message and don't fuck with me."

"Gladly." He continued his laughter. I had to ram him harder into the wall.

"Talk!"

"Victor sends his love," he sputtered.

"Does he now?"

"He says he'll fuck your girlfriend first before he eats her. The same way he fucked Henry's wife right in front of him before he cut off her foot and ate it."

My hands stilled, and I lost my grip on the fool.

God. In. Heaven.

No.

No.

No.

When I'd managed to get to Henry, Victor had him hanging from the ceiling of the old mental home in some sick game where he had to try and swing across to his wife, Lydia, to save her. Her left foot had been gone.

I remembered the ghostly pale look on her face as she'd tried to hold on to life.

Below them had been the two children. Victor had strapped a bomb to the them. I thought I'd saved the kids, but I didn't. I didn't save any of them. To hear that more evil had happened before I got to them was heartrending.

Fucking Victor. This was how you got to a guy like me. By messing with my mind.

Screwing with my mind. I wouldn't have known that Henry had to endure all that and Lydia had to go through that.

In my head, the image of them on their wedding day popped up. I would never forget how happy they'd looked. I'd never seen two people happier in love together. Then they went and surprised me more by being even happier when their children were born.

I would have loved to tell my friend that I, too, had found that one woman to steal my heart. The woman who could change me into what I'd probably wanted for myself all these long years.

But Henry was gone. Victor had shot him in his head, and Lydia, and he'd fed their children poison. All were dead.

Poor Lydia. That woman had been beautiful in every way and had loved Henry with her last breath. Victor had raped her.

It wasn't often that anything brought me close to tears and madness. But this...

Jesus Christ.

I wouldn't have known what really happened. I

wouldn't have known because in my book, no one had lived that night to tell the tale. Just one person who I'd thought was dead.

Victor.

I zeroed in on my new friend feeling the last shred of humanity slip away from me.

I raised my gun and pulled the trigger. The fool cowered against the wall when he saw that. He was, however, still laughing from whatever drug he'd taken.

My hands shook, and I realized that if I killed him, that would be ending him mindlessly. Self-defense was me. Self-preservation was me.

This was part of the game. I hated that Victor could know me so well.

Fucking bastard.

I was about to release the trigger when I suddenly imagined Amelia's beautiful face. Days ago, when we were at my place, I'd talked about changing. Then it became evident that I couldn't, but that was different to this. I wasn't telling her I couldn't change for her. I was saying I needed to do whatever I could to protect her, and I would.

I saw her beautiful face looming before me in my mind's eye, and it stopped me from pulling the trigger.

Instead of firing the shot I was nigh of releasing, I turned and walked away, letting the fool live.

However...

My years of experience kicked in. That clicking sound.

Click-clack...

That was all I needed to hear. I snapped around quicker than he could release the trigger and fired a bullet straight between his eyes.

Self-defense, self-preservation.

It was different.

I watched him go down. His eyes rolled to the back of his head, and he crumpled as blood gushed from the wound.

I took out my phone and called the number for the cleanup crew.

CHAPTER 6

Amelia

I didn't think he would answer the phone.

It rang out the first time and went through to voicemail. I could have given up and left a message, but I needed to speak to him.

Sinclaire needed to hear what was happening from me, what had happened.

I called again, and that was when he answered on the second ring.

"Taylor?" His voice sounded strange, faraway, and the name Taylor felt odd, reminding me of the fact I'd been a lie to a man who truly was my friend.

"Sinclaire, it's me, yes." The last time we spoke, he'd told me he was done with me. He found out about Luc, knew he was basically a fraud, and then came to my house only to find Luc leaving.

The worst thing was that the night before, Sinclaire had kissed me. My head was as crazy and foggy now as it was back then. One thing that was certain though was, I needed to bring the skeletons out of the closet.

"How've you been?" he asked.

"Not that great. Can I talk to you?" I sat on the window ledge in my bedroom and gazed outside looking at Dante and Gio, who were walking around on the front lawn. More guys were called in on the premises after Victor had been sighted.

"We're talking, aren't we?" Again, he sounded so distant and cold. It was understandable.

"Sinclaire, a lot has happened over the last few weeks. More than that."

"Tell me about it. It's been awhile since Roose approved vacation leave for three members of our team to be away at once."

God, that's what he thought.

"Yes, it must be hectic." I didn't know what the hell to say next.

"It's pretty quiet with Jefferson and Holloway gone."

Gone.

They were dead. Both of them, and I didn't know how I was supposed to tell him that, and shit, anyone could have been tapping into this line right now and listening in. I could put him in danger by saying too much.

I never thought this through. I released a slow thoughtful breath and ran a hand through my hair.

"Sinclaire, please take care of yourself." That was the best that I could say.

"What? You called me to tell me to take care of myself? That's rich. Are you shacked up with the mobster?" His voice boomed across the line harsh and raw.

"Please, take care of yourself, and if you don't mind, could you check in on Gigi?"

"Amelia…" That was strange, him calling me that too. He never did. "You sound weak… What's going on?" He knew something was wrong.

He knew me well enough to know when things weren't okay. It was nice to know that even when he was mad as hell with me and probably wanted nothing to do with me he still cared.

I paused for a moment to contemplate what I

could say to him. "I never told you this. But I think you're the only person I ever truly trusted wholeheartedly. I never told you much, but I didn't need to. I don't even think that I trusted Max or Gigi the way I trusted you."

"What's going on? Has he done something to you?" Worry was heavy in his tone.

"No, he would never. I just need you to promise me you'll take care of yourself." I thought of something. We had a code from when we were in trouble but dealing with the situation. "Be like a golden eagle riding on a horse."

He went quiet knowing instantly what I meant. "Amelia."

"Goodbye, Brad." That was his name.

I hung up before he could respond and turned to put my phone back in my bag.

I froze, though, when I saw Luc standing in the doorway. Hurt washed over his face. Hurt and something else I couldn't describe.

I didn't need to be told that the hurt on his face had to be down to him catching what I'd said to Sinclaire. I didn't know how long he'd been standing there, but I knew he must have heard that last part.

He must have heard me, must have heard every word I'd said to Sinclaire.

I knew the part that would have gotten him the most. It was when I'd said I trusted Sinclaire wholeheartedly.

My conversation wasn't long, but it was enough.

Luc walked up to me. The phone started ringing in my hands. Sinclaire was trying to call back. I placed the phone on the bed, and we both watched it ring out.

Luc reached out and cupped my face. Looking deep into my eyes, he looked like he was searching for something. Then he dropped his hands to his sides.

"Pack a small bag." He breathed ragged.

"What? What happened?" Something had happened. "Did you find something? Victor was here."

"I know, goddess. Please, just pack a bag."

"Where are we going?"

"I need normal. I need normal for a few hours. I need that with you. I can't... Please, just pack a bag."

What happened to him?

He looked me over, and his bottom lip trembled.

"My dad. I need to see if he's okay." I pointed to the door.

"He'll be fine. Someone will stay here and watch the place."

"You said we should stay here, you said that—"

"Fuck!!! Fuck, Amelia, please," he cried. "Just pack a fucking bag and come with me."

If I was worried before, I was scared now. Luc had never spoken to me like that before, and he'd never looked like this either. What came next shocked me even more.

A tear ran down his cheek, and he quickly wiped it away.

"What's going on in here?" Claudius asked from the door.

He looked in at us, gun at the ready.

"We're leaving for the day," Luc told him. He turned to face Claudius with a sneer on his face.

"Leaving to go where, *Lucian?*"

"Home. It's where I'd have my girl with me if this shit weren't happening. We wouldn't be cooped up in here in Raphael's house. Fucking Raphael. Fuck him. Fuck him, Claudius. Son of a bitch, fucking son of a bitch always thinks he knows what he's doing, but he's wrong. This time, he messed with the wrong people, and we have to suffer."

"What happened?" Claudius asked in a controlled, even tone. I was surprised at the way he was able to keep his cool because clearly, Luc had cracked.

Whatever these guys had done had cracked him and made him lose it.

Luc opened his mouth to answer and closed it again. He started again and sighed. He then walked over to Claudius and stopped to rest his hands on the door frame.

Claudius placed his hands on Luc's shoulders and stared him straight in the eyes.

"What happened, brother? You tell me."

"Lydia, Henry's wife. A goon sent a message from Victor to me, letting me know Victor raped her first and made Henry watch. He made him watch that happen to her. Then he cut off her foot and ate it."

I had to press my lips together to hold in the shock that coursed through me.

Luc had told me what happened to Henry and his family. It was awful, and it made me feel sick, but this ...

Claudius looked thrown too, but he released Luc, and understanding washed over his face.

"I can't let that happen to my girl. It won't. He would have to kill me first. Cut my head off, and even then, I would come back to protect her."

More tears ran down Luc's cheek, and his words gripped me.

He was right in what he'd said earlier. They all were. This was above me, and it started with Dad.

It was above all of us because I didn't think anyone here was used to dealing with a psychotic madman who had the power to mess with a guy like Luc, and from the expression on Claudius' face, I could tell Victor had reached him too.

"Claudius, you're a better man than me, but I can't be helpless, not like this. I can't let someone I love die. You know what I mean. You'd do the same if it were her, if you could bring her back."

When Claudius nodded with understanding, I realized there was something they were talking about that I wasn't privy to.

"One night. Then you come back here." Claudius held up a finger.

"Claudius—"

"One night, and you come back here with your plan of what you want to do."

Luc sighed, looked back to me and reached out his hand. "Doll."

I picked up my purse thinking it was best to take it.

I moved to him, took his hand and looked at Claudius as Luc took me away.

He gave me a curt nod of reassurance that I held on to.

It was one that told me I needed to up my game too and be strong. Somehow, some way, I needed strength.

I watched Luc chop the vegetables and set them all out on the granite work top.

He'd done an assortment of sweet peppers, red onions, mushrooms, and olives.

He got to work on the dough he'd made earlier for the pizza. It had risen substantially from the yeast he'd placed in it.

"Perfect. That should go well on this." He slid over a bowl of homemade passata.

I watched him, looking him over, trying to assess his mood.

We hadn't really spoken since we got here.

Thankfully, but much to his annoyance, Claudius had come back here along with their father, Marcus.

They were on the other side of the house. I guess it was more appropriate to call it a separate wing. It kind of was. So, it was like Luc and I were alone.

"What do you think, goddess? Does it look like we need more basil, or I could add some chili; that would be nice. Let me add chili."

"I don't want chili." It did sound nice, but I wanted us to talk.

He'd been on autopilot the whole time and had me sitting here just watching him.

"You like chili." He blinked a few times.

"I'm not in the mood for anything hot now. Just make it plain. Add more basil."

He held my gaze, and those blue, blue eyes took me in with worry. I stood up, and he flinched.

"Where are you going?"

"To get the salad." I pointed to the fridge. "I could make salad."

I moved to the fridge and opened the door. There was a bunch of vegetables I could use in there, but I went for simple and grabbed a head of iceberg lettuce and a couple of heirloom tomatoes. Gigi always put those in our salads.

Warm hands slipped around my waist, and Luc pulled me flush against his chest.

"I changed my mind. I want you for dinner instead," he cooed against my ear in a harsh, rough voice.

I put the vegetables back and turned in his

arms. "You just spent over an hour fixing up for pizza."

"But you don't want it."

"I never said that, and I do. I love your cooking."

"At least that's one thing good about me, right? You love my cooking, and I'm like a dog with mange you can't cut lose."

"Why are you saying that?"

He released me and moved back to the counter.

"Luc," I prodded.

He looked at me, regarding me with that stern expression I hated. I decided I hated it because I couldn't tell what he was thinking.

"How was Sinclaire?" He sneered.

I'd been wondering when he was going to ask me about that.

"Fine."

"Yeah, is that right? I'll bet he just loved to hear his precious Amelia Taylor tell him how much *she's always trusted him wholeheartedly*."

God. I'd seen him jealous before, but this was him hyped up on jealousy and worry. It made him act irrational.

"Luc, he's a friend."

"You kiss your friends? Come on, Amelia, he

wasn't just a friend. When did you stop sleeping with him?"

I blinked several times and continued to stare at him. I couldn't talk to him when he was like this. No way.

It was better if we didn't talk.

Deciding just that, I turned and walked away. He caught me before I could go through the door, grabbing my arm.

"Let go of me." I wiggled my arm free of his grasp, but I stayed there in front of him.

"Don't go." Now he sounded scared.

"I can't stay here with you acting like some crazy person, and how dare you speak to me like that? Don't you ever speak to me like that again, or the way you did earlier. I don't know who you think I am, but don't do it. I hate it. I hate taking orders, and I don't want you ordering me around and asking me shit like if I slept with Sinclaire." Heat burned my cheeks, and my stomach clenched. "I didn't sleep with him, and if I did, it wouldn't have been any of your business because I wouldn't have done something like that when we were together. So, don't, and don't act like some saint, because you aren't."

He hung his head in shame and bit the inside

of his lip. "I'm sorry. I'm sorry. Loving you is making me crazy."

I couldn't believe I was going to say this, but I had to. "Maybe you shouldn't."

"I can't stop, and I don't want to."

"I don't want you to either, because I love you, and I can't stop loving you either. No matter what Sinclaire is to me, he's not you. Even when I knew you were the man I shouldn't love, I still loved you. I trusted him, of course, and yes, I did so wholeheartedly, but he never had my heart. I was so lonely trying to be someone I wasn't. It was stifling and unnatural to me. I had to toughen up and be this hard person I wasn't. Luc, I'm a ballerina. We love music, we love peace and serenity. We love creativity and inspiration. But I threw myself into a world of evil and violence thinking I could change the world and do my part to stop it. Maybe on some level I felt responsible for who my father was. It's hard to have all of that going on in your head and not have someone to trust. That is what I meant."

"I get it, and I won't ask you about him again. I'm jealous because he's everything for you I'm not."

"Like what? Didn't you just hear me?"

"He's a good man. I am not."

"Define good, because from where I'm standing, I'm looking at the person who would do anything to protect me. Even if it killed you." I knew that about him, and it terrified me.

"I feel helpless, Amelia." He sighed.

"Me too, but if we lose each other, what do we have?"

He reached out and touched my face. The touch sent ripples of energy through me, and I leaned into his hand.

"I can't lose you. I love you too much."

"And I love you. Can't we just... indulge in that?"

His eyes searched mine, and he nodded.

I reached up for his chin and guided him down to my lips, loving the feel of the sharp bone structure of his chiseled face.

We kissed slowly at first, then the kiss turned up a notch when he swept his tongue into my mouth and tangled it with mine.

The slight tug on my bottom lip made me melt and forget.

"Let's go upstairs." I pulled away, teasing, and smiled up at him. "But..."

"But what, goddess?"

"We forget, we leave all the worries inside this

room and become whoever the people we want to be upstairs."

"The gardener and the dancer." He smiled with longing.

"No... just Luc and Amelia."

His smile widened. "I get to be me."

"And I get to be me."

I gasped and smiled as he swooped in and picked me up, hoisting me over his shoulder.

CHAPTER 7

Amelia

The minute we stepped through his bedroom door, I got lulled into the ecstasy of being with him.

I willed myself to take on the impossible task of forgetting all the craziness that was happening around us. Everything was happening so fast, and these were probably the last few moments we would have together as a couple who was crazy about each other.

This was our normal, and since I could have gotten an Oscar for best actress in my role as

Amelia Taylor for the last close to eleven years, I felt that I could pretend for a little while longer that this was us.

I took my mind right back to about a month or so ago when Luc had first taken me to the ballet. That week was crazy. We couldn't get enough of each other. We even missed work, and when we were at work, we used to steal time away in the stationary closet. I was certain someone must have heard us.

I'd never behaved that way before with anyone.

Here I was again, ready to indulge in Mr. Perfect.

He was that and so much more for me.

Luc set me down on the bed and proceeded to take off my shoes. I giggled when he threw them to the corner by the wardrobe. Next came my pants. He tugged on my panties, and I had to smack his hands away at the memory of last night when he'd torn them off me.

"No, you crazy guy. I never really got to pack much of a bag and I'm not walking around the place with no panties in front of all these men."

"You're moving in with me when this is over," he said, looming over me with a wicked smile on his face.

"Am I? I live in LA."

"No, goddess, you *lived* in LA. You can visit your friends when you want, but you're here with me. Chicago here."

"Isn't me moving in supposed to freak you out?"

"Nah, it would freak me out if you said no. I noticed you're not saying no."

"I didn't say no." I didn't, and I wouldn't.

"So, then you're saying yes."

"You seem to be the boss of me, so I guess I'm saying yes."

At that he moved down to my panties, bit the edge, then tugged on the lace with his teeth. The sight was truly hot, and sexy.

His blue gaze flickered, then turned darker to a twilight blue. The sinful smirk that inched across his sensual lips made my mouth water.

I didn't think he would do it, but using his teeth, he slid my panties all the way down, down, down my legs. I didn't have to think hard to remember last night, and nothing on earth could make me forget how I'd felt. I craved it now, wanting the wild passion once more.

He shrugged out of his T-shirt and pants, leaving on his Calvin Kline boxers, but I could see the bulge of his erection fighting against the soft cotton.

I took in the masterpiece vision of him standing before me like a dark god ready to take me in whatever way he wanted.

His perfectly sculpted abs, the peaks and valleys of the dip of the muscles that lined his torso, and the tattoos.

The satisfied smile that danced on his lips as he looked at me spoke of hot, sexual promises that I wanted desperately.

He moved back to me and tugged on the hem of my camisole top, lifting it over my head as I sat up. Luc then undid the clasp of my bra and practically dove in to suck my breasts as they spilled out. I could never get enough of him, and he could do that to me forever.

I arched my back into his wild suckle, and we both fell back onto the bed. His lips soft and searching moved down my stomach and left a wake of fiery kisses that sizzled my skin. Sizzled and scorched me clean.

Down he went until he reached my core and licked at the sensitive skin of my entrance. When he pushed his tongue inside me and started licking, I knew this would be a replay of last night.

Just like then, he licked me in soft, even strokes

that made desperate moans fall from my lips. Mindless moans of passion and bliss left me as the heat of desire washed over my body in a cascade of waves.

I was close to the edge. Riding on the wave of emotion that gripped me.

Luc pulled back and looked at me. Now the blue of his eyes was much darker. Dark with pleasure and sin.

"Not yet," he taunted. "Hold it."

God, I couldn't. It felt like an assault of my emotions when I held it. I sucked in a breath and allowed him to continue working his magic on me. Licking, sucking, teasing the hard, sensitive nub of my clit.

Jesus, I couldn't take any more. "Luc, I can't..."

He smiled wider and pushed his fingers inside me, pumping furiously. Pumping and stroking, giving me a pleasure-filled torture.

"Come for me."

The breath fell from my lips as I let go and pressed my head back into the pillows so I could handle the scorching orgasm that tore at my insides.

I cried out, crying his name and panting.

"We'll do that again later," he promised. "Time to take you."

I shuffled upright and pulled in a breath. "Not yet. I want to taste you too."

I wanted to give him the same pleasure he gave me, and I hadn't done that in weeks. We always got to the stage where I was too weak from the endless pleasure he gave me that I couldn't move after.

His face lit up at my request and brightened even more when I moved to him. He stepped back, and I pushed his boxers down his legs, unleashing the length of his massive, thick cock.

I dropped to my knees and smoothed my fingers over the base of his shaft and stroked down the length. I couldn't help but watch in fascination as his face contorted in pleasure. It fascinated me that I could make a man like him feel that way. He ran his fingers through my hair when I licked the fat head of his cock and took him deep into my mouth.

"Fuck, Amelia. I live for this."

And I was eager to please him. I sucked and licked, working him as I bobbed my head up and down, licking him clean and tasting him. He blew out a ragged breath and panted, then held my head closer, so I could take him deeper.

His cock grew, straining toward me, aching for release. I felt it, but still I continued and sucked hard. The pained look on his face encouraged me to continue, and continue I did, giving my man pleasure and hopefully soothing his worries away.

I loved him with my mouth, and I loved the taste of him.

"I can't... God... fuck." He reached down and grabbed my arm.

I thought we would fall back onto the bed but instead, he moved with me to the wall and pushed me up against it. I managed to catch my breath before he lifted my leg and guided his cock into me. I was already ready for him, so my body welcomed him as he slid in. I wrapped my leg around him and slipped my arms around his neck, giving him better access to pound into me. But what was best about this position was the fact that we could kiss while we got lost in the fast rhythm of his pumps.

The assault of his lips on mine, the hard, rough strokes that rocked my body, the dark heat of passion that melted me. *Everything.*

I had everything, and in that moment, this was all I wanted. He was all that I wanted.

His thrusts increased to the usual pace I'd gotten used to with him, trapping me in the torment of ecstatic bliss as he rutted into me, the lean beauty of his hips thrashing against me.

Although I was filled with him and he gave me

so much, I wanted more. My body begged for more, demanded more.

I relished the sounds of us echoing through the room. The sounds of our sweat-slicked bodies slapping against each other. The sounds of our moans and groans so loud and demanding. The sounds of my heart hammering in my chest.

Faster and faster he went, fucking me, riding me, and that was it. We both felt it. That relentless pull of the raw, primal need that consumed us. I had to wrap both my legs around his waist and grab on so hard to his shoulders that my fingernails dug into his skin and left a mark.

The orgasm that took me grabbed him too. I could feel it. He strained, then pounded home, bursting into me, and my body shuddered, bucking and thrashing against his as we shared the release.

"Luc!" I cried, unable to hold in the emotion.

He cupped my face and reclaimed my lips, soul-kissing me and crushing me to him. Kissing the world away from existence. It all faded away, and love flowed through me like warm honey.

It was a repeat of the day before, as if we were living the same day over again.

I lay in Luc's arms relishing him, and he beamed down at me in adoration.

Neither of us wanted to leave the bed because leaving the room meant walking back into reality.

We'd stayed awake for most of the night, only getting the bare minimum sleep we needed. Then waking up to make love.

He sighed, and I watched the steady rise and fall of his powerful chest.

"I think we should leave." His voice broke into the gentle silence that had settled over the room.

"Five more minutes, please." I ran my fingers up to his jaw and over the shadow of a beard that had formed on his face.

He chuckled and eased himself up onto his elbows. "I mean leave for good. Just go away and disappear. We could go to Italy. We talked about going to Italy. We could live in the villa, or somewhere else, and no one would be able to find us."

My lips parted, and numbness filled me, because I'd played that game before. I ran away from home, from Chicago. I became someone else and in all honesty doing that ate away at my insides and suffocated me.

Running away, that was me. Running...

"Luc, I..."

"I know it's like before, but this time you have me. If we get you out of the country, you could be safer, out of danger. It's a good idea, isn't it?"

I nodded. It was a good idea. Leaving. I would be safe. I could disappear, but what would happen here? What about Dad?

When I'd left before, I had the safety net of him. He'd looked so frail yesterday. He looked like he was on his last breath.

"My father, Luc."

"He will understand and do what needs to be done." His brows furrowed. I didn't miss the harshness in his tone and I recalled all that he'd said yesterday about Dad. "I'm thinking leaving might be our best option. We can think about it, but not for too long. Maybe by tonight. Tonight we can decide."

"Okay," I breathed.

"Okay?" He actually looked relieved.

"Yes. We decide tonight."

"Let's get back to Raphael's and see what's happening. But I'll plan like we're going."

It was all so sudden.

We got dressed and got back to the manor by ten.

I was so happy to see Dad sitting in the living

room with The Four. Claudius and Marcus came back with us.

It was strange seeing so many in this room. Although it was big enough to accommodate a small party of people.

I rushed up to Dad and gave him a hug and kissed his cheek. He hugged me back but then looked to Luc.

"Don't you dare say anything to me about taking her away from here," Luc cut him off before he could comment.

"I wasn't going to. I heard what happened yesterday," Dad answered.

Instead of sitting next to Dad, Luc took my hand and pulled me over to the empty seats on the sofa. I noticed Gio's cocky smirk at Dante as they exchanged curious glances with each other.

"It's been several days, and we've come up with nothing," Dad stated.

"They're playing with us," Luc filled in. I could feel his rage toward Dad rippling off him.

"They're fucking with us, son," Dad stated boldly. He looked more like himself now. "We need to turn this town upside down. With the level of control I have over this city, I'm surprised we haven't found them yet. It's more than odd. It suggest they have help."

"The Salvatores and the Manellos," Claudius offered.

I didn't know who anyone was.

"No, not the Salvatores," Marcus intoned. "Tag killed their consigliere. They would never link up with him after that."

"But they might with Victor. He's a powerful man to keep," Dad continued.

A buzzing sound interrupted his next words. It was my phone.

I pulled it out to turn it off, but I stopped when I saw the unknown number notification come up.

Luc looked too and tensed.

"What if?" *What if it was them?*

"Let me answer it."

"No, maybe it's Gigi." My heart told me it wasn't.

I answered the phone, and everyone looked to me.

"Hello." I couldn't control the tremor in my voice.

"Amelia, long time no see."

Chills ran down my spine. It was Victor. It was foolish to wonder how he'd gotten my number.

"What do you want?" I tried to sound firm, like this man didn't faze me, but again I couldn't help it. Just thinking of all the evil he'd done turned my stomach.

"You have a visitor. Make him feel welcomed. I advise you all to hold fire." He hung up, and the line went dead.

"That was Victor. Someone's here," I spoke, looking at everyone.

The guys all stood up and reached for their guns.

The doorbell rang, and we all looked at each other.

My heart was pounding in my chest. I reached for Luc's hand on instinct, and he took it, gripping me tight.

"He said to hold fire," I spoke out to no one in particular.

Dad boldly started moving toward the door. I went to stop him, but Luc held me back.

It was Dante who stepped in front of Dad and held his hand up.

"No, boss, no. I'll go."

He left us, and thank God Dad listened. A few seconds later, Millicent emerged with tears streaming down her cheeks. There was a collar around her neck with a red flashing light in the center.

"Millicent." Again, I tried to move, but Luc held me back.

"Good, good, keep a leash on that one, Lucian," boomed a voice from the corridor. A man walked in. He looked to be the same age as Dad and Marcus, but unlike Dad, he stepped strong. Strong and proud. His dark Italian features were striking, as were his silver eyes. They matched the silver streaks in his hair.

Behind him was Dante with his gun trained on him. The trigger was pulled back, nigh on release.

As I studied the man's face, I realized I'd seen him before. I knew his face; it was the eyes I recognized.

Dad had kept me and Mom out of business, and the only person I remembered seeing outright was Marcus. I guess because he was Dad's most trusted friend, but this man…

As I looked at him, I instantly took a dislike to him outside of the situation, and the feeling felt familiar.

Images of him and Mom flickered in my mind. I must have been about seven or eight. I couldn't quite recall, but I remembered seeing them together.

They were in the kitchen, and I came back from… ballet early. Millicent must have gotten me from practice. I ran into the kitchen, and he had his hands on Mom.

He'd looked at me as I dashed in.

This was Tag… God, I knew him. I knew him.

He looked at me now and smiled.

"Eloise, you could be her, Amelia."

The way he looked me over, it felt like he was staring right into my soul.

Marcus moved and stood next to Dad, drawing Tag's attention to them.

"Hello, old friends, look at us back together again. The infamous three. Raphael, Marcus, and Tag. You two went soft on me. One of you betrayed me. It wasn't you, Marcus. You would never do what Raphael did. Like me, you have sons you love. I see they're both here. I wonder what mine would have looked like today if they'd lived."

"Get off my property," Dad barked. "I will kill you right here."

"You can, but if you kill me, your beloved Millicent will explode. Simple. That collar around her neck isn't a necklace you know. Or some fashionable accessory. It's a bomb."

Poor Millicent. She started to shake and tremble. My heart went out to her.

"What do you want?" Dad asked.

Tag laughed. "For those of you who just joined

in or need to be brought up to speed, my name is Taglioni Donachie. This man," he pointed to Dad. "*Your boss*, ratted me out to the feds on a heist we were supposed to work on together. He did that because his wife chose me over him. His wife chose me, and jealousy made him foolish and selfish. He ratted me out to the feds, and the stint cost me my three sons and his beloved wife. The love of my life, who came to warn me of the great Raphael's plan to ruin me. Then the evil man he is didn't stop there. He stole the very diamonds we were supposed to take together and got me out of town under the pretense that he was helping me. What a fool I was. So, here I am, armed with the truth, which I had to work out for myself, and this is what I want."

He walked right up to me. Luc jumped in the way, but Claudius grabbed him and held him back.

"Blood for blood," he taunted.

I swore my poor heart stopped beating right there in the walls of my chest.

"The daughter for my sons' and her mother's lives. And I want the diamonds."

He stared me down, but I stood firm and strong, immovable. My heart felt like it would leap straight out of my chest when it started beating again, but I calmed myself enough to stand up to him.

He stepped back and laughed. "When I get all those, I'll kill you, Raphael, before that cancer gets you. Death like that is too good for you. The real games are about to begin. I hope you're all ready," he sneered as he walked by Dad and Marcus and continued down the corridor.

It wasn't until I heard the front door open and close shut that I released the breath I'd been holding on to.

Millicent broke down, and I ran to her aid to comfort her.

I looked at the device around her neck, which snapped open a few seconds later.

"Go after him. See if you can follow him," Luc ordered Dante and Gio, who were already moving.

"We need to get rid of that thing." Claudius moved in and took the collar.

I looked to Luc wondering what the hell to do now. One thing was for damn certain. I couldn't leave.

I couldn't leave and leave my father again.

CHAPTER 8

Amelia

I sat with Dad for the longest time while everyone else got to work.

We were in the sunroom. We stayed in there for hours not really doing anything, not really talking.

I didn't know what to say to him, and I guess he didn't know what to say to me.

He read—or what seemed to be reading—a copy of *Scientific American*.

Occasionally, he'd comment. Nothing in relation to what happened earlier, just random things like talking about the vegetable drink Millicent had given him and the lunch. He said he'd become a vegetarian because it was healthier for him. The meals Millicent prepared contained anti-cancer properties.

By the time it started to get dark outside, I'd had enough of the small talk and shit, and I hadn't seen Luc all day.

Dad and I were like sitting ducks waiting for the real games to begin.

"I saw him with Mom," I spoke, cutting through the thick silence that made the room heavy with tension.

Dad lowered the magazine and stared at me with wide eyes. "What did you say?"

"I saw him with Mom. I was maybe eight, I think, and they were here in the kitchen. I got back from ballet early. I rushed into the kitchen, and he was there holding her. I think he was about to kiss her when I barged in."

Dad closed his eyes. The revelation highlighted that Mom's affair had gone on for a lot longer than he'd thought. It must have stemmed over many years.

"I'm sorry, my girl. I'm sorry you had to see her

like that, and I'm sorry I was no much better and my actions put everyone in danger."

"Luc wants to take me away," I spoke in a hushed voice, just above a whisper. Aware that someone could still be listening in.

"It's a good idea."

Of course, he would say that.

"I shouldn't leave you. Again."

"The focus is you. I thought you'd be safer here with people who could protect you, but I was wrong. I was so wrong. Tag was the most ruthless man I'd ever come across in my life. What I did to him probably made him insane. I'm still, however, trying to figure out how he put the pieces together. It's still a mystery to me. No rat would have been able to tell him what happened because no one else knew what I'd done. To everyone, it looked like I was getting revenge on Eloise and trying to get Tag out of the feds' reach. I played along well."

He ran his hand over the stubble on his chin and looked drained.

"Dad, you need to go rest. Go and lie down."

"I've been lying down for days."

"It's where you should be. Come, let me help you upstairs." I moved to him and took his arm.

He smiled and stood up, towering over me

with his height. "This is more than I deserve, my daughter."

"Dad, please stop saying that."

I got him upstairs and made sure he had a mug of hot cocoa, then I went back downstairs to check if Luc had come back. I needed to speak to him.

I found Claudius instead. He was in the living room sitting by himself. Still looking over the collar that had been on Millicent's neck. I felt so bad for her, and for the fact that she was caught up in all this shit. We'd sent her home after that whole fiasco, escorted, of course, to make sure she and her family were safe. She'd told us how they'd grabbed her from her house. Her husband was away running some errands for their grandkids, so she'd been by herself.

"It's funny. This really was just a necklace," Claudius said as I approached.

"Not a bomb?" I pressed my lips together.

"They fooled us big time. It's just a wireless controlled device with a flashing light." He tossed it on the table.

"Could they listen in with it?" I sat opposite him in the loveseat.

"Nah, it's not that sophisticated. It really is just a worthless piece of shit." He motioned his head to me. "So, you and Luc decide what you're doing? I thought you would have headed for the hills by now."

"He told you?"

He shook his head. "Didn't have to. We almost have the same mind. Let me guess. He wants to take you away from here."

"Yeah."

"You don't think it's a good idea?"

"Do you?"

He swallowed hard. "I'm biased, so I can't answer that question."

"How?" I wasn't sure what he meant.

"Well, it's because I would do the same thing if I were him. I would do it in a heartbeat."

Luc had said that too, to him, last night. They'd been talking about someone. "Would you?"

"I tried to... for my wife." He looked down, then back to me, and his eyes spoke a wealth of sadness.

"You were married?" Luc never mentioned that, but I guess maybe the story behind that was one he'd rather not tell.

"I was. I made a deal with the devil, and things went south," Claudius began explaining. "I was supposed to secure a deal. A million-dollar deal for the Manellos, but it didn't work out. I work as a bookie in the business, and I thought I'd make a little extra on the side by throwing games and other shit. On this occasion I didn't know what I was getting myself into. They linked up with a psycho who wanted to steal one of those sophisticated chips that could hack any system. My part fell through and lost them their chance. I took my wife away because I sensed something would happen, but it seemed that I had a rat too because they found her and killed her. I don't want to guess what they must have done to her first before death came. Where she was staying was supposed to be a top-secret safe house." His gaze fell to the floor then climbed back up to meet mine.

My heart was full. There were so many bad stories floating around this house.

"I'm so sorry. I... I can't imagine what you must have gone through."

"Thank you. So, hey, I'd run too if I were Luc. This cross is for her. The men in my team have the same for the ones they lost. For me, it was my wife. Dante, his sister. Gio, his father. Jude and Alex are brothers. They wear the cross for their older brother."

I stared at him, not quite knowing what to say. "There's all so much."

"What do you want to do?"

I shook my head. "I don't think running is the

answer. I did it before for different reasons, and I hated it. I can't do it again, and my father needs me."

"You'd be safer away from here." He pointed out and lifted his shoulders into a shrug.

"Would I? They found me in LA. There's nothing to stop them from finding me wherever I go in this world. And how long would I be gone for? Running and hiding. I don't want to live like that. I want to stay and fight."

He smirked. "I figured you'd say that."

"Really?"

"Yes, I guessed from the way you stared down Tag. I knew then that you weren't going anywhere."

"Blood for blood, right?" I offered.

"Blood for blood."

Luc

I felt bad that I'd basically flipped out over the last few days.

My sense of calm was shot, and I was on the verge of losing my mind.

Yesterday, after Tag made his appearance, I went with the boys to hunt for him.

We came up with nothing, but I suspected they knew that would happen.

I was starting to believe that one of the other crime families was definitely helping them out. Same way we had our alliances.

They had bigger friends than us though, most likely people who wanted to take Raphael's power.

It was probably perfect for them. Cut the head and work your way down, then dive in for the taking with what's left behind.

I just couldn't believe that we couldn't even get a glimpse of them, except for when they wanted us to see them. That was it, part of the fucking game again.

We'd only see them when it was time to play.

I got back in the early hours of the morning and slept in the chair next to Amelia. I didn't get in the bed because I didn't want to wake her. She needed her sleep. She needed to rest, and she'd definitely looked exhausted yesterday.

I hated that Tag got up in her face the way he did, and I hated the things he said to her. But she took it. She stood bold and faced him.

I was proud of her.

I woke up before her and walked over to her dressing table, where I noticed she'd taken out some of her stuff from the past and set them on the top. There was a pair of ballet shoes. Satin pink Bloch pointe shoes with pink ribbons attached to them. Next to that was a button that said *Made at Julliard*. It was one of those quirky little buttons people collected.

My heart sank when my gaze landed on a few pictures of her. She couldn't have been more than fifteen or sixteen, but damn, she looked like she was made to dance. The picture was of her dressed in a white tutu with diamantes on the bodice inserted into the pattern and a headband made with white feathers. I think this must have been her in Swan Lake. She'd told me about this. I remembered how her face had lit up as she spoke.

She looked so different. Beautiful, very beautiful, and I could immediately see that if we'd known each other back then, I would have been in trouble because I would have pursued her and gotten my head blown off if Raphael had caught me.

It was such a shame that she never got to live her dream. So much talent gone to waste, but maybe I could salvage that somehow. If it was possible, I would do it.

I would do it in a heartbeat.

I picked up the ballet shoes again and smiled, imagining her wearing them.

"I don't think those would fit you. You could try them though." Her voice pierced through the silence that had settled over the room.

I turned to see her sitting up in bed. Her hair was braided to the side in one of those complicated patterns, and she wore one of those camisole tops that drove me insane.

"I won't damage them." I chuckled, setting the shoes back. I moved to her and looked her in her eyes.

Warm honey came to my mind, but the troubled look that lurked in them gave me the answer to my question from yesterday. I knew she wouldn't want to run away with me.

Thinking back now, it was foolish of me to suggest it because we weren't dealing with people who didn't know what they were doing.

We were dealing with people with the know-how to do anything and get dirt on you, you thought was shelved.

Meeting Tag, I more than ever wanted to know how he'd found out about what Raphael had done. It took me back to my theory that it was by accident. I'd always thought it was an accident somehow, but I couldn't put my finger on it.

"I was looking through some stuff last night. You were gone for so long."

"I'm sorry, and I'm sorry I flipped out. I shouldn't have lost it like that the other night, and I've been this irrational bastard ever since."

"It's okay. Luc..." She brought her hands together, and I knew she was gearing up to tell me she wanted to stay.

I reached out to take her delicate hands and held them up to my lips to kiss her knuckles. "I know, goddess. You don't want to run."

"It's not that I don't want to run away with you. It sounds so romantic. But we don't know how long this will take. We don't know if running may make things worse, and I doubt we could just do that. You guys seem really good at what you do, but I noticed that Tag and his people seem to appear when they want us to see them."

Woman after my own heart. "My thoughts exactly."

"You aren't mad at me?"

I shook my head. "No, goddess. I'm more annoyed at myself because I didn't think this through. It's kind of crazy too that every single plan we've come up with over the last few days has been nullified." It was everything. The plan to get the diamonds, the plan to hunt, the plan to leave.

"I know. It's because they want us in this game of theirs. Tag's plan. I get it though. The whole thing about blood for blood. My father took away everything from him, and he wants revenge. It's as simple as that. I just don't want to run anymore, and this time if I ran, I'd be looking over my shoulder. We could never really be happy."

"I know." That was true. We'd always be looking and waiting for someone to find us. It would be no way to live.

"I can't leave my father either. I can see it now. They'd find out we left and kill him straight away. I know he's done so much wrong, but he's my father. Luc, he's my father, and he's dying. For my own peace of mind, I can't leave him."

"I understand." I kissed her knuckles again and thought of what we'd spoken about in relation to her moving in with me. "I'm still holding you to moving to Chicago."

"I know you are." She smiled. "I forgot to ask you why we couldn't just move to LA. I like my house by the beach. We first kissed on that beach."

"I wanted to do more than kiss you on that beach."

"Yes, I remember very well."

I pulled her into my lap and admired her smooth golden legs. "You want me to go to LA, I'll go. I hate it there, but I can love it for you."

She ran her hands over my jaw and leaned down to kiss my nose. "I never hated Chicago. You love Chicago, and I think of it as home. We like Italy too. I think I see me here."

"Yeah?"

She nodded and smiled. "Look at us. I think we're planning the future."

"I like that. I want it with you, but you must promise me one thing."

"What's that?" She searched my eyes.

"Dancing. You have to find yourself. You have to promise me you'll find a way to do what you love most. You might not be able to go to Julliard, but you mentioned teaching, and I'm certain you can still dance if you want to. Just find a way."

She nodded, and it warmed my heart.

However, a buzzing sound made my heart shy away again. It was her phone on the nightstand. A text had just come through.

She looked to it and froze but moved off my lap to look at it.

I watched her pick it up, tap in her password,

then her hands started shaking and she screamed, dropping the phone.

I jumped up instantly and picked it up.

On the screen was a picture of Victor with Gigi. Gigi's face was black and blue, and around her neck was the sign *Player 1*. Victor had a big smile on his face, like he was taking some fucking selfie.

CHAPTER 9

Luc

"I'll live. I'm just waiting for some meds, and then I'm on my way," Maurice told me. He coughed, and it made a static sound on the phone.

He'd taken a bullet to the chest. It grazed the side of his chest, but I knew he couldn't be okay. Not okay enough to be on his way. I would have preferred for him to stay in the hospital.

"You need to stay."

"Luc, this is one time I'm not listening to you. Fucking idiots used knock-out gas to get in the house. They took my girl and killed all the men who'd been standing guard, but it seems like they wanted to keep me alive."

I sneered hearing that. Victor was one damn son of a bitch.

"It's all part of this fucking game."

"Oh yeah, I don't doubt that one bit. That bastard left me behind to tell you what happened. I saw the gas and instantly knew what was going down. Gigi was in her room reading her cards and casting some protection spell over the place. I'll tell her it didn't work when I see her."

I'd known Maurice long enough and well enough to know that when he joked about something like that, it meant he was deeply hurting.

"We'll get her back," I promised. I knew over the last few weeks from our conversations that he'd taken a shine to Amelia's friend. Gigi, the good witch who could charm anyone. They'd better not hurt her.

My brain was numb because I knew that if Victor had her, anything could happen to her. We'd tried calling the number the text came from, but to no avail. We'd also tried tracking it with our contact from the CIA, but nothing. The number wasn't registered to anyone, and there was no trace on its location even though the phone was supposedly switched on.

The first thing I did was call Maurice when we got the picture of Gigi, but I couldn't reach him. I'd panicked, but hours later, he'd called back and explained what happened.

"I'll get her back." Maurice broke into my thoughts. "I can move, and that's all I need to do. I got my flight booked already."

"Maurice, you took a hit to your chest. It's crazy. You should at least stay the night."

"I was here last night. It's enough. The bullet grazed just near my arm, so it's no biggie. I've been stitched up, and like I said, I can move. See you soon, bro." He hung up.

I'd been standing in the hallway. Everyone else was in the living room.

I went back in to find that Amelia was still crying. She was sitting next to Raphael, and Millicent brought in a tray of cookies.

Claudius and Dad stood by the window looking out.

"What did he say?" Amelia asked.

"They were ambushed with knock-out gas, and Gigi got taken. They shot Maurice and killed everyone else."

"Luc, this is getting ridiculous." Claudius chimed in. "We have to find them somehow. We need to find out who the hell is helping them and get to the bottom of this."

"Yes, and I'm coming," Amelia offered.

"No, you aren't," I said before she could continue on that tirade.

"She's my friend. This happened to her because of me. It's Gigi, Luc. You know what Victor is capable of. Jesus Christ." She started to cry again, and Raphael placed his arm around her, pulling her close to him.

He looked beside himself with worry and hadn't said much. Of course, what could he say?

This... all of this wasn't fucking happening because of Amelia. It was happening because of him.

I walked up to her and took her hand.

"Amelia, I promise you I'll get her back." I didn't know if it was wise for me to make such a promise, but I'd die trying. That was more of a possibility.

A phone rang. No buzzing this time. It took me a second to realize it was my phone.

I pulled it out, and there was the unrecognized number we'd been waiting for.

"Victor," I roared into the phone, not bothering to wait to confirm who it was.

"Oh, Luc, what if I'd been someone else? Like

your hairdresser or dentist, or florist or pharmacist. I would have gotten a most terrible fright with you yelling at me like that."

Amelia stood up. "Give her back, you son of a bitch!" she screamed.

Raphael stood too and took hold of her arm.

"Tell her she's right. I am a son of a bitch. My mother was absolutely a bitch. She was a librarian at a boarding school for orphans. I lived there, and it was terrible. She hated me because I was the spawn of some loser, like it was my fault I was born. Ha, ha, ha. She shaved my head and used to cut me every time I was bad. She made me sleep in ice water if I didn't get my times tables right, and damn, would she ever whip me with her cat of nine of tales if I didn't say please or thank you. Do you know what she did, Luc? She killed my so-called father and fed him to me. My first taste of human flesh. I think that kind of messed me up, you know. She was the first person I killed. Didn't eat her though. Not her disgusting flesh. Didn't want the taste of her in my mouth."

It made me sick. It made me physically sick. I couldn't even be sympathetic to whatever the fuck kind of messed up childhood he must have had.

Victor was Victor, and I didn't care. What I

cared about was what he'd done, and what he was currently doing.

"Victor, give Gigi back. Give her back to us. She isn't part of this."

"Are you kidding? Of course, she is. She's the best friend. In this game, I have your girl's bestie. Last time it was yours. She's starring in that role in this movie."

Amelia started shaking. I was pretty certain she could hear what he was saying.

"What do you want? What the fuck do you want?" I cried.

"Oh, Lucian, this isn't that kind of call. I don't want ransom just yet. We have to get to the arena first and play this game out. Forgive me. I should have said I wouldn't be saying 'Give me Amelia and the diamonds in exchange for Gigi.' This call was just to fuck you up even more. You can't find me, and only God knows what I might be doing to the beautiful witch. Maybe the same thing I did to Lydia. She has very pretty toes. Matches her hair. She's my kind of woman too."

I made the mistake of covering my mouth.

When Amelia saw that, she looked worse. I couldn't help it though. It was a natural reaction because of all the horrific images that coursed through my mind.

"Victor, please leave her alone." I was begging. I was begging a fucking psychotic animal, and all he did was laugh at me.

"Oh, behold the great Lucian Morientz, capo to the Rossi family, underboss, boss of them all, begging. Ha, ha, ha, ha."

Amelia burst into tears.

"Victor—"

"Lucian, if I were you, I'd worry about the next player in this game. In the meantime, I'll give Miss Gigi the star treatment."

A second later, a tortured cry of desperation and anguish sounded. It was so loud it hurt my ears.

It was Gigi screaming. It was her screaming from what sounded like the depths of her soul. We all heard it.

Amelia crumpled to the ground in floods of tears. Then the line went dead.

Amelia

Numbness…

Numbness gripped me.

It gripped me, and I couldn't ...

Couldn't think, couldn't focus, couldn't breathe.

What was the point of me? I was a cop. I'd left my best friend in the care of a mobster while I fled to Chicago to more mobsters for protection.

Okay...

All of that was wrong, and for all my time in the organized crime unit, I didn't use the knowledge I'd gained.

Fuck, for all the time I'd been a mobster's daughter, I didn't use the knowledge I'd gained from that either.

Your enemies come at you through your weaknesses.

What were weaknesses? Loved ones.

The answer was simple. My loved ones were my weakness, and like any other well thought-out plan, this was the same thing.

What a brilliant plan too. Earlier, when I'd told Luc I understood Tag's quest for revenge, I never really thought about what I was saying. I was talking as a person who hadn't really been hurt yet.

Cole died because of me. That hurt me to the

depths of my soul. Sinclaire nearly died too because of me.

Gigi though...

God, was she dead? That scream sounded like she died. That scream sounded like she was being tortured to death, and I couldn't imagine the pain she must have gone through. Been going through.

Luc took me to my room, where I lay down on the bed, processing what was happening and what was going on.

I would have gladly gone to them in exchange for Gigi. Gladly and effortlessly. But Victor probably knew that.

Right now, as hard as anyone had tried, no one knew where he was, and we were just supposed to wait.

Luc had been sitting in the little chair over by the window watching me. He didn't say anything; he just watched over me. When Dad came in, I rolled onto my side and cried even more. I was barely able to ask them both to leave. To leave me alone.

I knew Luc felt terrible. Dad did too, but right now, I didn't want to be around any mobsters.

I didn't want to be around anyone like that who could hurt me, and my friends.

Gigi...

I remembered the day when I'd met her. Back at college.

I was so scared to take the leap of going somewhere I'd never planned to go. I was basically alone in the world, and it had felt like she was this angel who was sent to watch over me. She'd helped me adjust to the shock of being alone and at college. A place where so many changes happened in your life.

She was there for me, and we were such great friends that we'd continued living together. Our stupid rule was, we'd move out when we found the right guys to take care of us.

Neither of us had until now.

Me... at one point, I thought I'd move on with my ex, but being with Luc had taught me that I didn't know what the hell love was until I met him.

But this... this way of life was going to kill me. The poison would start in my soul and kill me slowly once it consumed me.

That's what tonight felt like. Like toxic poison, killing me slowly, and the longer I waited, the worse it got, the more it worked its way into me.

The door opened, and I lifted my head. I didn't want to see anyone. Not unless they had something good to tell me.

The person I saw though was the exception. Millicent. She wasn't a part of this whole fiasco.

I sat up and looked to her. As always, whenever I was sad, she brought me a tray of her signature cookies. Cookies and milk.

It didn't matter how old I got, she did that for me, just like she was doing it now.

"Miss Amelia…" She attempted a smile, but it weltered. She moved to my side, set the tray on the nightstand, and sat on the bed next to me.

"Millicent, I can't bear it. I can't bear it."

"I know, sweet girl. I know. You have endured so much."

"I don't know if it's right to say that I endured it. I feel so week and weary, and I can't believe what's happening."

She reached out and touched my hand. "I know. I don't know what to say. All I can say is, maybe we can hope. Maybe we can hope that she's still okay and we'll save her." She nodded and looked so sad.

Concern and sympathy flickered in her eyes, and she picked up the plate of cookies. She held it out to me with that soft smile again.

"You have to eat. Keep up your strength. It looks like it might be one of those long nights again. Luc and his brother are gone out looking.

They took The Four. I don't really know much, but it looked like they were ready for war."

"Where's Dad?"

"In his room." She held my gaze. "Luc got some guys to stay with us. Eat and drink, Miss Amelia, please. Don't let me have to worry about you starving."

I took a cookie and nibbled on it. I wasn't hungry, but I thought I'd eat it for her.

Since I was thirsty, I took the milk and downed it. The soothing coolness of it was refreshing. I finished the cookie and was about to reach for another cookie when the plate moved.

The plate...

It shifted in Millicent's hands. Shifting from side to side, then it became a blur.

What the hell?

I blinked several times trying to focus, but my head...

It felt so light... like feathers floating in the wind on a gentle breeze.

My mouth and throat now felt dry and like I couldn't move my lips.

"Millicent, what is..."

Millicent started crying. "I'm so sorry, Amelia, I'm so sorry."

Even though I was looking at her and she was

talking, I didn't know what she was saying sorry for.

It was foolish... oh so foolish. *Trust.*

It was foolish, because really, in the end, the only person you can trust is yourself.

When the door opened again and Tag walked in smiling, I started to shake. I willed my body to move, but I couldn't feel my legs.

Tag...

Millicent...

Tag...

Millicent... the milk... the cookies.

"You look so much like your mother." Tag beamed, lowering to cup my face. "Eloise... it's like I'm looking at you all over again."

I glanced at Millicent feeling the tears run down my cheeks. "Millicent? It was you. You did this."

Those were the last words that slipped through my mouth before the darkness took me and my eyes rolled back in my head.

CHAPTER 10

Luc

~

I'd resulted to my lowest.

I didn't care who I had to kill anymore to get information.

The situation had just become next level bad, and I couldn't sit around waiting.

No way.

No fucking way.

So, what did I do? Or rather, we...

While my other guys were searching the streets, Claudius, myself, Saul, and The Four headed to the home of the Fontaines. They were the highest up on the order of crime families who wanted to end the Rossis.

The plan was to try them first, then the next in line. The Salvatores. We were going to our enemies, jumping straight into enemy territory on dangerous grounds that could get us killed on sight.

For who they were, they didn't have much protection at the door, but then again, maybe they were relying on who they were to keep people out.

We shot the lock off the front door and kicked it wide open.

The butler ran away, and another guy came up to me, foolish enough to try and stop me, but I sent a headbutt straight to his forehead, knocking him to the ground.

When we barged into the sitting room, Antonio, the capo for the Fontaines, looked like he was about to shit himself. He was a guy as tough as me, but I could and would beat him to a fucking bloody pulp if I had to.

He was in the middle of getting a lap dance from what looked like a cheap hooker.

Fucking bastard was married and had four kids. Men like that made me sick to my stomach. The hooker ran out when she saw us, and Antonio reached for his gun, but I shot the damn thing out of his hands before he could get a grip on it.

Claudius grabbed him around his neck and hoisted him up in the air. Dante reached for his shotgun and aimed it at him, and Gio took out a long reach knife.

Saul just smiled at him, revealing his silver teeth.

I walked up to Antonio and stared him down hard.

"Victor. You know who I mean. Where. Is. He." I roared.

"I don't know." Antonio literally looked like he was going to combust with fear.

"Gio, cut something off," I ordered.

Gio moved to him with his knife, but Antonio cried out, and his red puffy face turned brighter.

"Wait, please," he begged.

I loomed in closer and sneered at him. "Do we look like we're here to play with you, Antonio?"

"No. No."

I pulled out my gun now and pressed it to his chin. "Don't fuck with me. I will blow your brains out now if you don't tell me what you know."

"Word... word on the street is, the Anotenellis and Barattas are helping them."

Fuck, my blood ran cold hearing that. Those

families were literal assassins. I didn't know how a guy like Tag could have any connection with them, but right now, that wasn't for me to work out.

"Where are they hiding out?"

"I don't know, Luc. I actually don't know. But... I suggest you keep her close, as in right next to you, if you don't want them to find her."

Her.

He knew about Amelia, so that meant they all did.

Damn it, the phone rang again.

I reached for it instantly and answered fast when I saw the unknown number.

"Victor!" I bellowed like a raging animal ready to charge and kill.

"You did it again," Victor taunted.

"Stop fucking with me."

"Don't worry, sunshine, I will. The players are all here now, in the next game you get to still try and find out where we are." He laughed a maddening, sickening laugh that reminded me of the Joker in Batman.

The players...

What does he mean? The players.

"Who are the players, Victor?"

"Come on now, Luc. I thought you would have guessed. Henry was your best friend; you came for him. On this occasion, as planned, I thought I'd act out of the goodness of my heart and get Amelia. She doesn't need to worry her pretty little head over where we are. Oh no, no, no."

My eyes bulged and I couldn't blink. I released a sharp breath as shards of cold fear washed over me, like knives piercing through my body. I shook my head in disbelief.

My nightmare.

My worst nightmare actually happened. Tremors took my hands and sweat made the phone slippery in my hands even though I was gripping on to it.

"You have Amelia!" I could barely speak and just managed to whirl around to face Claudius, who released Antonio instantly.

"Yes, that's what I'm saying. I got your girl. Again. This time was so much easier. You all scampered away guns blazing, leaving the rat in the house. Don't you know you should do your best to get rid of vermin? God, Luc, makes me wonder what your kitchen looks like. I don't think I would eat from you."

"Don't hurt her. Don't you hurt her."

"Luc, you know how this goes. I always hurt them. Come on, I'm Victor Pertrinkov. I don't want people to think I've gone soft. Oh no, no."

"I swear to God, Victor, if you hurt her—"

"You'll what, Luc? What can you do? Couldn't save Henry, couldn't save Lydia, and you couldn't save their kids. Have you ever saved anyone?"

Bastard. Once again, he knew how to get to me.

"Just give her back, give them both back. There must be some humanity left in you. I'll give you anything, anything." Begging again.

"Tell you what, if you could be a dear and grab those diamonds, that would be awesome. It would save me from getting it. I already got paid a billion dollars for this job, and I'm a man of my word. I get hired to do a job, and I do it well. It's good for business. People leave good reviews. I want five stars in all categories." He laughed again.

"I'll get the diamonds." Claudius looked at me when I said that.

"Good, little boss, you get the diamonds, and I'll tell you when to get to the arena."

I closed my eyes as my heart shied away from the craziness. I couldn't believe what was happening. I just couldn't believe it.

He took Amelia...

He had my girl.

~

Amelia

Something burned my nose.

Something that smelled really bad. Like sulfur and shit.

My nose burned and stung from the inside, and my head felt like it would fall off.

Where am I?

I lifted my head. Big mistake.

Ugh. Why was it hurting?

I went to reach up to touch my forehead, but my hands... they were bound behind my back.

Tied up with what felt like thick ropes. I was able to run my fingers over the twines.

The room, or wherever it was, was dark. I couldn't see anything. There was a light that flickered in the corner. Looked like a candle.

It grew bigger and wider in appearance.

Then there were footsteps.

The outline of a man appeared before me, and as he came closer and held the candle right in front of his face, my heart jumped into my throat.

Victor.

He got me. He caught me.

God. This was it.

As I remembered everything and Millicent's betrayal, bile rose into my throat. It rose into my throat, and I couldn't stop myself from vomiting.

"Shit, couldn't you have warned me you were going to do that?" Victor winced. "This suit is expensive."

When I threw up again, I realized it couldn't have been from the realization of what had happened. I was sick.

I was actually sick…

Whatever Millicent had given me had made me sick.

Did she poison me?

"Vomit is so gross." Victor frowned and stepped back, so he wasn't near me. At least that was one good thing. Anytime spent where he wasn't touching me was a good thing. "God, and nasty. Burt, send someone in to clean that up, will ya," he called over his shoulder.

"What did you give me? What did you people give me?" If it was poison, I could die. Just like that. Mission accomplished.

"It's an anesthetic, similar to what's used in hospitals prior to surgery. Major surgery. I should give you a list of the side effects. The only real thing you can do though, I guess, is the throw it all up."

"Where's Gigi?"

"Lights." He held up the candle like some kind of freak, and bright white light snapped on from above, filling the room.

Instantly, my gaze landed on Gigi. She was directly opposite me but about six feet away. Duct tape was covering her mouth, and she was bound just like me, but she was alive. Alive but what appeared to be sleeping or knocked out.

I didn't know. What I knew was, I could see the slight rise and fall of her chest.

There were bruises all over her face.

Tears ran down my cheeks. Tears of sadness because I couldn't believe that my poor friend was caught up in this mess, but also tears of relief. I thought the next time I'd see her would be...

Well, I thought she was dead.

"Don't look so relieved. I have much in store for you, Amelia Rossi," Victor taunted.

I returned my gaze to him, looking over the madman that stood over me.

"Why? Why are you doing this?" I didn't care what he was getting paid. This was pure evil. He was pure evil.

"I get a kick out of it. Anything like this is me. Come on, how many times do you think I get to have this kind of fun, Amelia? It's a hoot and a half. Plus, what can I say? I love my job. Oh, also, maybe there is this." He snapped open his shirt to reveal his chest. I winced at the sight of the angry-looking burn scars that covered it. "Those scars make it personal for me. Women cringe at the sight of it. The way you're cringing now. Doesn't help much in the bedroom."

I couldn't imagine what woman in their right mind would be with him, but then maybe they didn't have a choice. Again, bile rose in my throat when I thought of what he'd done to Henry's wife. And all he'd done to Henry and his kids, the whole family. Plus, there were more people. I didn't know Henry and his family or the other people this man had hurt, but that didn't matter. None of that mattered. This was the man who'd done so much evil. So many people had lost their lives and had their lives ruined because of him.

He cleared his throat and continued talking. "Your boyfriend did this to me. Took me a long while to heal, but like Rasputin, the mad Russian monk, I came back from the dead. I trust he must have told you what happened between us. That little explosion could have killed me if I'd been deeper inside the building. However, it was good for people to think I was dead. It was more dramatic this way, plus it gave me time to get to a hundred percent. Probably better. I lost a lot of clients though while I was down. I blame Lucian for that."

"You're crazy."

"Newsflash, people kind of know that, as do I, my love." His eyes went wide with excitement.

My mind ran on Dad and Millicent. What did they do to him? Where was she? Where was Tag?

"My father. What did you do to him?"

"Absolutely nothing. It's not his time yet. This is the main event. He's probably at home tucked in bed watching shit and reading the Bible. Poor asshole, as if reading the Bible can help him. Can it help anybody? Hardly, even when you do what the good book says, you're still at a loss. He seems to take comfort in it. I wish I could burn it right in front of him. I'd have fun doing that. I'd torture him then too."

He walked around swinging his head from side to side like he relished the thought. I took the opportunity to look around the room. Anything that could give us some escape would be good. Of course, providing I could get out of these bonds. The room we were in looked like an old-style interrogation room. Like something from *The Green Mile*. Large space, bars ahead of us with a door. It made me think we could be at the old, abandoned prison. I couldn't remember the name of it, and there was a good chance we weren't there. I stopped looking around when Victor turned back to face me with a devilish smile. It was a smile a predator would give its prey. He looked at me like he wanted me to answer. What the hell kind of answer should I give him?

Anything I said would most likely infuriate him. I couldn't call him an evil, psychotic madman.

"Poor sap," he taunted, seeming to love the sound of his voice. "There's a chance he doesn't even know what happened to you. Millicent was such a good sport. Giving us all the information we needed, feeding us with data. Good woman. She wore a wire and everything, allowing transmit live and in living color to get straight to us. That's what you call a good sport. A real team player. She deserves an award or something. Best spy."

"How did you get to her?" I wanted to know. I had to know. I wanted to know everything.

"That wasn't me. So, your guess is as good as mine. She was already playing the game when I got on board. That wire of hers worked wonders though. Technology these days is off the hook. That little device allowed us to hear even the slightest whisper from thirty five feet away. Good right? We heard things even before she heard. That's how we knew about the key and the safe. Also how we knew when to get rid of the wire. You have to agree that nothing is sweeter than the betrayal of a friend. A trusted family friend who was more like family to you. We well and truly put her to good use."

God, I couldn't believe it. Of course it all made sense now. They played this game so well. They didn't need to bug the house when they had Millicent wearing a wire. She did indeed catch the tail end of the conversation I had with Dad in the garden. However, by then it was too late. Chances were she never heard any of what I'd said but they did.

They'd already heard me say that I was going to put the key in the safe. They may have even heard the whole conversation prior to that too depending on where Millicent was in the house.

That laugh sounded from him again, making me sick.

"You people will pay for this," I cried. It was stupid to say that, like I could really make them pay. I couldn't do anything. I was helpless. So much for being a cop. Look where it got me.

"Your beloved won't be able to save you." He laughed. "He thinks he can just get the diamonds and hand them over, then I'll let you both go. As if I've ever been a bargaining man. He'll come along riding on his white horse, and either I'll shoot him in the head and take the diamonds, or one of my lackeys will get him."

"Bastard!" I screamed from the depths of my soul.

"Once again, you are right. I was a bastard child. You seem to know me quite well. The thing is, Amelia, you are my prize. No money on earth can make up for the delicious flesh of a beautiful woman. And I get two for the price of one."

Oh God... God.

I had to will myself not to cry. What worked and stopped me from crying was watching Millicent come through the barred doors with a mop and a bottle of disinfectant.

My blood actually boiled.

She walked in, not looking at me, and started cleaning the area around me where I'd thrown up.

Victor laughed and laughed and laughed. Then he did the most disgusting thing by pushing her and shoving her to her knees. She cried out in pain, and it was then she looked at me.

"Cleean, cleean away like you're trying to wash away your sins." He made a show of spinning around and dancing. Arms out to either side while his legs did something close to what looked like a cross between the Irish gig and a Russian gopak. It was quite a spectacle.

However, while he did that, Millicent gave me a pointed look, flicked over her hand to reveal a little key, and wedged it in the crack in the floor board.

She squeezed her eyes shut and moved back before Victor could see what she'd done.

My heart started racing, beating a thousand beats per minute.

She was helping me.

"Cleannnn!!!" Victor cried.

Millicent cleaned, and I realized things weren't exactly as they seemed.

CHAPTER 11

Luc

There were no words to describe the feeling that washed over me when I went back to Raphael and saw the cleanup crew outside his house.

Inside and outside.

We'd left eight guys here, and only one had lived to tell the tale. The guy who lived was in a coma, and there was a chance he wouldn't make it.

I'd seen this before, several times, and I hated death. I hated it in every sense. Especially death like this. Mindless, useless killing to leave devastation.

While Claudius and the guys stayed with the crew, I went to find Raphael.

He was in his office sitting by the window.

In his leather chair, he faced the window, and I couldn't see his expression. From the slump in his shoulders I knew the weight he must have carried.

Amelia was gone, more people had died, and surprise, surprise, the rat in the house had enabled this mess.

Who was the rat? Well, I had a wild hunch now.

It grieved me to think it. It grieved me deeply to think it because if I was right—and I strongly suspected I was—I'd handed my girl over to the traitor.

Millicent.

She was the only person who should have been here and wasn't, and Victor didn't mention taking her. He hadn't said anything about taking her at all.

It still didn't add up, but there were pieces of this nightmare that were starting to fit. Some of the things the other knew could only have been delivered to them by someone who was close with us. They knew specific things. Too specific to guess.

Claudius was right. The butler or the housekeeper.

Raphael turned when he sensed my presence. He looked at me with the desolation I felt.

I closed the door and walked over to him, leaning against the window ledge, so I could face him.

Tears streamed down his cheeks, and he held a picture of Amelia in his hands. It was of her dancing.

"They took my child, Luc. I..." He rubbed his hands over his face, smearing the tears.

"I know." I hadn't spoken since we left the Fontaines. My voice came out in a rasp, and my throat was dry. I didn't know how I was even able to talk or give off this calm appearance I seemed to portray.

Truthfully, inside I was dying. I was dying, and I didn't know what to do.

Amelia, my Amelia.

What would that fucking Victor do to her? What would he do to her to get back at me?

This was the very thing I'd vowed against just the other day.

I should have taken her and fled the country. It would have been better than this. Running and looking over our shoulders for the rest of our lives if that's what it took would have been better than this.

They took Gigi, and I didn't even know if she was alive. Chances were, she wasn't.

So, my first duty should have ben to protect Amelia at all cost.

It was funny how this had all started.

Money and power, that was what this was about. Money and power.

Falling in love wasn't part of the plan, neither was finding out I was just a pawn in Raphael's game.

A person to be used. And I didn't even want the damn business anymore. I didn't want it, and it was almost laughable... I didn't want this life either.

At first, I'd told Amelia I'd change for her, but she wanted me to change for me.

I wanted that too, now more than ever. Life was more than this. Life was more than greed and wanting more money, more everything.

My life used to be get laid and get paid, get paid lots and have the finest women at my beck and call.

I shed that man I used to be from the minute I set eyes on Amelia. Right there in that restaurant as she arrested Montgomery. Then, in the weeks that followed, I took the time to get to know her, and she trusted me.

I trusted her.

I had to trust myself now to get her back. To get her back in whatever form Victor would give her to me. And... I knew he wouldn't just hand her over either.

He'd mentioned *arena*, and I knew the games were just starting.

It was like some damn battle to the death.

"Millicent," Raphael breathed, dabbing his eyes with a tissue.

I nodded. "She's the rat, Raphael, has to be. I can't think of anyone else who it could be. It fits. She's not here, and there's no mention of her."

"Yeah. I have to confess that I suspected her after those guys broke into the library. There were no tapped phone lines, no hidden crevices for anyone to hide and see Amelia put the key in the safe in the library. Amelia and I were talking about it in the garden, and it was then I gave her the key and told her the password. She said she'd put the key in the safe in the library. At that moment, we saw Millicent, but I thought she'd just come up to us. I didn't realize she must have been there long enough to hear what we were saying."

"Jesus, Raphael, why didn't you tell me that

before?" Once again, he'd proven to be an asshole. Had he voiced his concerns with me, his second most trusted advisor, we could have put more eyes on Millicent. We could have stopped her from coming here.

He winced and shook his head. "It's a hard thing to accuse someone of something like that, especially when it's a trusted friend. Luc, she's been in this family since before Amelia was born. I took her on to help my wife when she was pregnant with Amelia. She's looked after Amelia ever since. It was her who came and alerted me to my wife's affair with Tag. Why would I think she would betray me like this?" He shook his head again and wiped more tears away. "There's no way that I could conceive that someone like her could betray me, not like this. So many have died because of her hand in this. Helping them."

"Why do you think she did it?"

"I don't know. I've sat here going over the whole thing in my mind. I knew it had to be her because of tonight. If you guys had been here, they wouldn't have come. You, Claudius, The Four, Saul. God, even if Marcus had been here, they wouldn't have set foot on the premises."

Pa was at home. Claudius had called him on the way here. As far as I knew, he was on his way.

"They knew we weren't going to be here, and the only way they knew that was by someone telling them," I filled in.

Raphael nodded.

The idea was to take the best, and if we got Victor and a chance to get Gigi back, we'd take it, but to do that we needed the best. That damned Victor must have known we'd retaliate after that last phone call. He knew this would happen. He knew I would go after him. He knew I would fail.

We'd played right into his trap.

"Someone told them, and I realized the only someone that could have been was Millicent. The sick thing is that I was here when all this shit was happening, and I couldn't do anything. I was asleep in my bed; my meds knock me out when I take them. Millicent usually brings me up a glass of juice before she leaves. I woke up thirsty and decided to go downstairs to get some water. That was when I saw the bloodbath. When I went to check on Amelia, she was gone. They took her right from underneath my nose. When I pieced it together, I abandoned all that shit about long-term family friends, and fucking shit. I knew, I knew it had to be her. It was all too nicely played for it not to be. Specific."

At least we could agree on something.

"Victor wants the diamonds, Raphael."

"In exchange for Amelia?" He looked hopeful.

"He didn't mention anything about an exchange."

Raphael bit the inside of his lip. "He just wants you to get the diamonds. Then what?"

"Well, that's the part I need to work on. I won't give him anything until he gives me Amelia and Gigi."

"It won't work that way."

"I know, Raphael, but right now, you're going to give me the details I need to get the diamonds." I was past showing respect. It was time to start demanding.

"Of course, of course, I will give it to you."

"Raphael, I don't know how this is going to play out, but we need help."

I'd thought of that on the way here too. This was bigger than us. We couldn't find Victor or Tag. They had the assistance of the worst people I knew, and that made them one step ahead of us.

"I'll call in resources. I'll get everyone I know."

"While I'm gone, I need you to work on finding out where the fuck they are. I can't sit here and wait for Victor's call. It will be too late then. It will be far too late, and God knows what he'll do to Amelia. It might already be too late."

"Please don't say that." His eyes displayed a wealth of soul-wrenching sadness that mirrored my own.

"I have to be realistic, Raphael. I have to, which is why I'm asking for help. We can't go to wherever he is by ourselves. We need guns. We need muscle. We need anyone you can think of who can help. Good and bad."

He nodded. "Okay. When are you leaving?"

"A few hours, so I can get to the facility when it opens." Rockford was about a two-hour drive from here. "Do you know opening times?"

"Nine o'clock."

Great, I would get there for then and be ready for action.

Tomorrow. Tomorrow had to be the day this nightmare ended.

It had to be the day when I killed Victor once and for all. No more games, no more shit, no more messing with my mind and the people I loved,

Just no more.

If I made it and saved Amelia, we'd leave. Leave this life.

Put it all behind us and start fresh. We'd leave just the way she did years ago.

Claudius insisted on going to Rockford with me.

I refused his offer because I wanted time to think, but when I got to the facility, that seventh sense of mine kicked in.

Felt like we were being watched.

Amazing how I could always sense trouble. Trouble at its fullest and finest.

But I was stupid to think that Victor or Tag would just allow me to get the diamonds and wait to be told what to do next.

Claudius and I were checked before we were allowed inside the facility. We handed over our guns. Unknown to the guards, however, was that we each carried pocket knives that looked like a key holder.

And we had our fists.

We were led to the vault by a large bald man with a scar on his face. Didn't exactly look like a guard for a place like this that housed antique paintings and family heirlooms. As far as I knew, there wasn't money as such kept here, but there were gold bars and diamonds.

Claudius and I had exchanged glances when the guard first approached us. The look in Claudius' expression told me he was thinking the same as me. That we needed to be ready as hell for an ambush once we got our hands on the diamonds.

The guard stayed outside the vault when we went in.

"Luc, I hear footsteps," Claudius muttered under his breath.

There was shuffling just outside the vault door.

"Me too." I typed the password into the keypad on the panel outside the glass case, and it opened. The case opened first, then another layer opened, revealing a little silver box. It was the same size as a jewelry box. I'd imagined it to be bigger, but I guess it would be the contents inside that would make up the volume. I grabbed it, snapped it open, and widened my eyes.

I'd heard about these diamonds. Imagined that they would be what royalty of olden days used to wear, and not just any old royal either. These diamonds were very rare, and their value was always prevalent.

The box was full. I knew I held a few billion in my hands. All this trouble for these little things.

Claudius looked at them too. "Jesus Christ, I could only dream of the wealth contained in this box." He chuckled and tucked a lock of his hair behind his ear.

"Who wouldn't?" came a voice from behind us.

It was the guard, and he had company. Three tough guys had joined him.

I snapped the box shut and placed it inside my pocket.

"Can I help you with something?" I asked in a cool, even tone, rocking back on my heels like I didn't have a care in the world.

"The diamonds, please." The guard put out his hand. The other guys walked up to us. Claudius started laughing.

"Really, you think you can take us?" Claudius challenged.

That was when more men walked into the room. Ten of them.

Fuck, we were fucking outnumbered, but no way in hell was I going to let this end here. These fuckers would get theirs.

I sprang into action when one of them fired at me and two rushed at me. I landed a kick in one guy's throat, snapping his neck. The other I gave an uppercut and grabbed for a headbutt that smashed his nose in and cracked his teeth.

Several men rushed Claudius, but my brother held his own and fought like a demon.

We worked our way through eight of them in a mass of punches, kicks, and finally, I grabbed a gun and was able to kill the guard.

But fuck, more guys came in. Like the plague. One fired a shotgun that split the bullets out in several directions. I almost got hit, and Claudius pushed me out of the way.

We both dove behind the stand that had held the diamonds to take cover.

"We need to get out of here. Just focus on retreat," Claudius cried.

When we stood up, more guys were in the room. Another ten of them.

I didn't know if we were going to make it. I couldn't let them take me. A really tall ex-military-looking guy rushed me, and I kicked out at him, but he whipped out a kick to me too, throwing me off balance. I fell, and he grabbed me. I sent a knee to his balls, but it did nothing. Claudius was fighting, giving his best, but there were too many of them.

The hulk of a guy holding me pulled out a gun and held it to my head.

He laughed. "Lucian Morientz, people will remember me for killing you." He pulled the trigger.

That *click-clack* sound pierced through me because I thought this was my last moment.

Amelia

I love you...

My last thoughts. I'd love her with my last breath. It was like slow motion. I was sure I saw him release the trigger, but his hand blew up. Something pierced his hand, and blood spurted all over my face.

I fell to the ground and looked ahead in disbelief as I saw Maurice come in guns blazing. Beside him were Sinclaire and a guy I only knew by picture to be Max. Max, Amelia's old partner back in LA.

Holy fucking hell.

They came in like vengeful gods firing shots. Shooting until all the goons were dead.

CHAPTER 12

Luc

Sinclaire walked up to me as I stood and landed a fist straight in my face. He would have done it again if Max hadn't held him back. Maurice just shook his head.

"Fucking asshole," Sinclaire cried, looking at me with death-filled eyes.

I didn't say anything or retaliate because he was probably right to do that. In his book, I'd stolen his girl and put her right in the arms of danger.

"Cool off, man," Max told him. "The last thing

we want is to get in trouble here. More trouble. The kind that could get you benched from the precinct."

"Cops, Maurice?" Claudius asked with narrowed eyes and a deep scowl. He hated cops worse than me.

"They're not just cops; they're Amelia's friends." Maurice was right, and these were possibly the help I needed. They loved her and had her back. They may hate me, but they loved her.

Having them here gave me hope.

"Still cops."

"Cops that came to your rescue, asshole," Max retorted. He looked to me, and a lock of his dark hair fell over his eye. "Where is she, Luc?"

"Taken," I replied, looking at Maurice, whose shoulders fell on hearing that.

"We'll get her back," Maurice said, sounding positive. I had to admire him for it.

"Taken!" Sinclaire cried now looking feral. "You! This is your fault, you fucking gangster. All you did was mess everything up. Why couldn't you just leave her alone?"

"I don't have time for this, Sinclaire. I need to focus on getting her back. We can argue all you want then. Not now."

"She called me and gave the code. I knew she was in trouble."

I didn't know she'd done that. I'd heard her speaking to him, but I didn't know anything about a code.

"What code?"

"Golden eagle riding a horse. It means I'm going through deep shit, but I'm dealing with it."

"You came based on that?"

"Of course I came. I had my bags packed and got Max back when I heard about the shootout at Amelia's place."

"Then I got involved and asked them to come," Maurice said with a nod.

Didn't matter how they got here. They were here, and they'd saved our asses.

I looked from Sinclaire to Max. "Help me get her back." Maybe it was the way I said it, but it seemed to throw Sinclaire.

The last time I saw Sinclaire, I practically had my hands around his throat.

Now, I'd take help wherever it came from. Anything to get Amelia back.

"If anything happens to her, I'll kill you." He pointed at me.

Claudius tensed.

All I did was look at him, then proceed to walk through the door.

He didn't know that if anything did happen to Amelia, I wouldn't want to go on living.

When we got back to Raphael's place, there was a rather interesting woman waiting for us inside.

She was an addition to the team that had come from LA. Her name was Cora, and she was a high-tech hacker. Max explained that the LAPD had used her for a number of special secret projects.

At first, I didn't think much of her because she had purple hair and seemed more at home in a cyber bar at college, but she surely put me in my place from the minute she opened her mouth.

Apparently, she thought she could track Victor's location from the number that was on Amelia's phone. The number he'd sent the text message from with Gigi's picture. Thankfully, Amelia's phone was still in her purse and hadn't been taken with her.

I tried to tell Cora that we'd already tried to locate him this way, but she was still of the belief that she could do it.

It gave me some hope. Hope I hadn't felt since this whole nightmare took off.

We all sat in the living room, and tension was thick in the air, to say the least.

Cora sat near the coffee table with a laptop in front of her. Sinclaire and Max stood side by side behind her. I sat opposite her with Maurice and Saul. At least we were near them.

On the other side of the room were Raphael, Pa, Claudius, and The Four. They kept to themselves, and the looks they cast this side was enough to kill.

Cops and mobsters. Cops, mobsters, and one tech hacker.

Maurice had brought him and Max up to speed with what was going and who Amelia really was.

Neither of them had asked me about it. While Sinclaire was very vocal, I noticed Max said very little. I'd never spoken to the guy, and knowing him for the hour or so I'd known him, I didn't know what to make of him except that he didn't like our kind. I guess I had to understand since Raphael had threatened him to take his family and uproot to Florida to make room for me to slip in as Amelia's fake partner.

I'd become a cop, a thing I hated most. Back

then. My tolerance had grown substantially over the last few months.

"I think this should work," Cora announced. She glanced at me and looked away instantly. Her skin flushed, and she looked uncomfortable.

I didn't mean to look the way I did with the harsh expression on my face. And quite frankly, I didn't care how I looked. My concern was whether or not she could help.

"What are you doing?" I asked.

"More than you," Sinclaire muttered under his breath.

Fucking asshole was working my last nerve. He kept dropping remarks like that the whole time. Like this was all my fault.

"What's that supposed to mean?" I looked him straight in the eye, and the fool looked back at me. It didn't help that he was standing and I was sitting down. It made it look like he had the upper hand over me. Authority.

"Go figure." He smirked.

I glanced at Claudius, who leaned forward with a grin on his face. It wasn't a grin of amusement; it was the expression he wore right before a fight.

Of the two of us, I was considered the more

even-tempered brother. Claudius wouldn't stand for this shit.

"Go figure?" Claudius challenged. His voice reverberated across the walls.

Sinclaire looked at him. I felt jealous of the wary look that washed over him, because he seemed to be more afraid of Claudius than me.

Saul started laughing.

"This is real interesting," Saul commented. "Cops and mobsters. It's like a game."

"Can we just keep quiet, so Cora can focus?" I offered.

Again, she looked at me, nervously, but she faced me.

"I'm screwing with their firewalls."

"They have firewalls on a phone number?" Never heard of anyone doing that.

"Yeah, big time. They hired the best to do this. It basically stops any trace from being made on them. Very clever."

"This is what you call resourceful," Sinclaire intoned, still with that taunting.

"We have resources too," I informed him.

"Looks like they did fuck all to me."

"Right, you know what, Sinclaire, you can go fuck yourself." I'd had enough, and this pissing contest was breaking my cool.

"Easy, guys." Max put out his hands to both of us.

"Yes, easy, I need to concentrate," Cora said, tapping away at her keyboard. She was purely focused on whatever it was she was doing.

On her screen were a bunch of codes that looked like something from *The Matrix*.

They all ran down in lines. I didn't understand what any of it meant, but I had to hope that her belief in what she was doing would work.

I needed something to work. Something more than the nothing we had going for us.

If it worked, we'd have the upper hand. We'd have a mission to plan. I was certain Victor would know by now that we made it out of the facility, but maybe we had a little bit of time and leeway. It was a wild guess, and me hoping we did.

Cora straightened suddenly, and the code started unscrambling.

"Eureka." She beamed.

"Eureka, as in you found them?" I stood up and moved closer.

"Yes." She nodded her purple head excitedly.

"How did you find them?"

"Virus. I just hacked their system with a virus, and they actually won't know." She tapped away at the keyboard again and instantly, I saw a locator triangle hovering over the map.

She zoomed in.

"Peyton Prison," I said before she could.

Why was I surprised? The place was abandoned. It had been for years, but damn, it was a secure prison for the worst criminals. The ones with severe psychotic tendencies. The kind of place Victor would go apart from hell.

It was almost déjà vu. With Henry, Victor had taken him and his family to an abandoned psychiatric hospital of the worst kind. It had been closed down for its inhumane practices. Peyton Prison was basically the same.

"Peyton Prison," Cora confirmed.

"Alright, let's go." I crackled my knuckles.

"Wait, not so fast." She held up a hand.

"What?"

I was very impressed with her skills so far, and I'd be putting it mildly if I said I was simply eager to get going. However, the woman impressed me further by zooming right into the room the phone was located. She hovered around the screen, tapped her keyboard, and the inside of the facility came into view.

"What did you just do?" I asked.

"I tapped into their CCTV, so I can see what's happening inside."

I moved closer to her. "Can you see Amelia?"

Raphael stood up now and made his way over.

Cora clicked on a series of codes and stopped when we saw Amelia. My heart jumped in my throat. She was in a hall like room tied to a chair, looking around.

Maurice gripped my arm as we looked at Gigi, who was also tied to a chair.

She looked pretty bad with her bruises, and she hung her head down, looking limp. Her eyes were closed. She looked like she was in a bad way, but alive. Thank God she was alive. As long as she was alive, I'd save her.

Cora looked at both of us.

"God. Sorry to move from this screen, but I saw something a few screens back."

As she switched the screens, my heart ached. *My Amelia.* I let those bastards take her.

Cora switched to a screen that brought up the foyer, and I saw instantly what she meant as she zoomed closer.

The floor had little devices all over it. Little balls that looked like Christmas decorations.

"I don't know what those are, but you might

want to be careful of them, and that." She tilted the camera, so that it showed the ceiling.

"Holy shit," Max breathed.

There was a big axe-looking blade the size of a man hanging from the ceiling. It looked like it was connected to some trip wire.

"Victor said we'd be going into an arena," I stated.

"Well, these look like traps to me. All of it." Cora bit the inside of her lip.

"How will we get in?" Raphael asked.

"I'll check something out." Cora switched the cameras to outside the facility near the lake. There was a tunnel where water gushed out. She looked over the entrance and nodded.

"The surveillance stops past a certain point in the prison. Looks like the old section has nothing. If you can get in through there and work your way across to where they are, you could go unnoticed. I'll try and find the best entrance to get in. I suggest going in different teams. Surprise is a good advantage, and having a backup plan."

"Okay, rally up the best men we have. They're team B, and we are A," Raphael declared.

I looked to him and cleared my throat.

"We?" I cocked my head to the side and arched a brow.

"Yes, we."

"Look, sir," Sinclaire cut in. "I don't know if Amelia would like it very much if you put yourself in danger."

"I appreciate your concern and you both coming here, but she's my daughter. I'm going to get my child back."

"Raphael." I wrinkled my nose. It was insane. He couldn't come.

"Lucian, don't... don't." He held up his hands and stared me down. "Give me five minutes. You guys get prepped."

All I could do was stare at him. He sounded more like the man I was used to.

It was just a shame he looked so frail, and that just might get him killed.

CHAPTER 13

Don Raphael

10 years and 11 months ago...

"Make sure you get it done just the way I said. You need to be there at the right time to get them, catch them in the act." I couldn't keep the anger out of my voice, or the hurt.

How was I supposed to?

Four nights ago, I caught my wife cheating on me. I actually saw her. I actually fucking saw her with my own two eyes.

Millicent had warned me. She said she saw Tag and Eloise in the park and they looked really friendly. Too friendly for her liking. Suspiciously friendly. Millicent hardly wanted to tell me, because the accusation was so serious.

She warned me, but I wouldn't listen. I wouldn't hear of it because there was no way that I would have believed that Eloise would do this to me. To hurt me and our family like this.

Things were bad between us, but damn. Damn it, I didn't think they were so bad that the problems couldn't be fixed. I didn't think they were so bad that she took refuge in the arms of another man. One of my best friends.

Tag... I couldn't begin to express the disappointment I felt about him. And the hurt to my heart was unbearable.

"I have everyone ready," Agent Peterson replied with a sigh.

He was my contact with the feds. He'd helped me out a number of times and was a good associate to the business. Of course, I paid him well for his services, so he couldn't exactly complain. He had the best of both worlds. He loved being a fed, but he also loved money. Who didn't?

"Raphael, this is Tag we're talking about. He's

not like you."

"What the fuck does that mean?"

"He's not as reasonable as you. He's hot tempered and could retaliate. Can you seriously see him cooperating when we arrest him? He's the kind to fire back and run."

"You're a fucking federal agent. You don't allow the other guy to run from you. You know Tag, and come on, if he gives you trouble, you know what to do. Shoot the fucker."

Yes, shoot the fucker. I was done with that guy. I'd known him for so long I couldn't remember not knowing him. I would have trusted him with my most precious possessions. My wife and daughter.

I kept Eloise and Amelia out of business, kept them right out, but the two guys I trusted most were Marcus and Tag. Marcus met both Eloise and Amelia. When he moved to LA, Tag stepped up and became my consigliere. My confidant. A confidant and friend I trusted enough to introduce to my wife. I introduced the two right here in this house. We had him over for dinner one night. It was just the three of us while Amelia had a play date with her friend from ballet.

When he met Eloise, the two got on well, but I didn't realize I'd just set in motion a train of disaster for myself.

That one meeting, just that one meeting years ago sealed my fate and crippled my marriage. I didn't know how many more times the two met after, or when this affair started and became full blown because I didn't have Tag back here after that. All I knew was it happened. Eloise came by the office a few times and would have seen him. It would make me crazy trying to figure it out. Trying to pinpoint the when and the where.

"You want me to kill him?"

"You kill who you have to."

I seriously hoped this guy wouldn't cross me the wrong way. Not today. He could come with his bullshit some other time, but not today.

This was the perfect plan. It couldn't have been more perfect.

The diamonds were coming in on the shipment, smuggled in from South Africa. Tag, his three sons, myself, and a few of my guys were supposed to be there to collect. The plan was to set up and go in for the taking once the coast was clear. We'd been planning this for months. Before I knew of Tag's deception and betrayal.

We'd checked times for when we could pull off this heist in the stealthiest way. Well, plans changed four nights ago when I watched him pounding into my wife.

I still couldn't believe it. I'd followed Eloise, and she'd gone to Tag's place. I snuck in the back and watched. I watched them together out of shock and horror. *Sadness.*

"You do what you need to do. Get it done and make sure there are no loose ends. He'll be getting to the docks in about half an hour. Follow the directions I gave you."

"Okay. I'll check back in later."

I hung up.

It was her reflection in the window that startled me, her in that red dress, that made me whirl around to face her.

Eloise was standing in the doorway. Tears were streaming down her cheeks, and sorrow filled her beautiful face.

Shit.

I thought I was alone in the house. No one was supposed to be here. She said she was going shopping.

I would have taken more care in my conversation if I'd known she was going to be here.

"Raphael, what are you doing?" Her voice shook as she spoke, and more tears ran down her cheeks. "Did I hear you right?"

Damn it, I was such an idiot. I'd allowed my feelings to cloud my actions, and I didn't think. I should have made that call back at the office. Not here.

It was so ironic. I'd kept my wife and daughter out of business, kept everything at the office in town. I'd kept things tight and on a leash, never discussing anything in the house, yet she'd just heard me plotting perhaps the biggest and worst ambush I'd ever concocted.

"What did you hear?" I demanded.

"Tag. You just ordered Agent Peterson to kill him if he had to. He's your friend. Why would you do that?"

That was it. I lost my composure. "I saw you with him."

I was never a beat-around-the-bush kind of guy. Never. And I wouldn't start being one now.

Eloise sucked in a sharp breath, and her skin turned pale.

"W-what?"

"I. Saw. You. With. Him!" I screamed.

"Raphael, please, I can explain." She rushed up to me.

When she tried to touch me, I moved my hand away.

"Why? Why would you do that? And what kind of explanation do you think you can give me? You slept with him. I watched him with you."

"You watched?" she gasped looking mortified.

"That's what you're concerned about? Well, yes, Eloise, a person tends to do crazy shit when they're in shock. That was one of them. Though it was more the case of me watching in complete horror and disbelief because I didn't want it to be true. I couldn't believe it. You and him. Don't worry. I left before he finished fucking you."

"I'm sorry. I'm sorry. Raphael, things haven't been... I should have come to you and told you I wanted a..."

Wow, please, don't tell me she was going to say what I was thinking.

She swallowed hard and wiped her face. "I want a divorce."

"Done. Fucking done." Of course, I was done. Didn't matter that I loved her with everything in me. Didn't matter that this was killing me. I was done.

If she didn't love me. I couldn't do anything about that.

"Raphael, things have been bad with us for a long time."

I wished she hadn't said that. "Yes, that's the perfect excuse to go fucking my best friend, right? I understand perfectly. That's the natural thing to do, of course."

"It's not. It was wrong of me, and I made a mistake."

"I would never do that to you." I had plenty women who would have been eager to be with me because of who I was and what I was. I owned Chicago, I had unimaginable wealth, and I think I could be bold enough to say that I owned people too. There were so many chances for me to cheat, but I would never. I didn't believe in it, and I was too in love with my wife to even contemplate hurting her like that.

"I know. I know you wouldn't, and that's what makes me feel even worse. Raphael, every time I tried to talk to you, you'd come up with some excuse or take us someplace that would make it inconvenient to tell you how I felt."

I couldn't deny that I'd been stepping around a fear I didn't want to acknowledge. I'd felt at one point that she wanted to leave me. I'd felt it, and it terrified me. It terrified me so much I didn't even want to acknowledge the fear. So, I'd pushed it aside.

"How do you feel? Tell me, Eloise. I have given you everything. I have protected you from the darkness in my world. I have given you my heart and soul and loved you."

Her lips trembled, and she shook her head

slowly. Her face contorted as she winced and pulled in a sharp breath. "I don't love you anymore."

I just stared at her. I stared at her for what felt like an eternity, and I was sure that my heart must have stopped beating.

"You don't?"

"I'm sorry."

I had to fight back to control my own tears. "I love you." It was stupid to say it, but the words fell from my lips mindlessly.

"Raphael, I'm so sorry. I don't love you. I don't love you, but that doesn't mean I don't care about you or appreciate all you've done for me. You've given me everything. A beautiful life I would never have had if not for you. Our precious daughter... but... I just... I lost that connection we had along the way." She nodded. "Please don't kill Tag."

"Do you love Tag?" Again, another foolish question. I never asked a question I didn't already know the answer to, and I'd just landed myself in the shit of that one.

She blinked several times, and her lips parted. "You don't need to know that."

"Because it's true. You love him." In rage, I grabbed the glass weight on my desk and threw it against the wall. It smashed, and she shrieked.

"You can't kill him. Please call off whatever plans you have." Her bright eyes pleaded with me. "Please.

I could give her a divorce, but I wouldn't give her a divorce and see her with Tag. Tonight, Tag would either end up in prison for a very long time, or dead.

I answered her with a smile and stepped back.

"Raphael, please," she begged.

"No, noooooooo." No a million times. That asshole would get his if it was the last thing I did. "No!" I cried out and my voice was so primal and feral I didn't recognize it.

Her eyes went wide with fright. "Bastard, you'd kill him?"

"Not like I haven't killed before."

"I hate you. I hate you." She turned around and ran through the door.

I didn't care.

As far as I was concerned, I'd lost her. I wished to God I could say that I hated her too, but I was cursed with loving her. Loving a woman I'd been with for nearly twenty years. We had our beautiful Amelia, and I'd thought we were the family I always wanted.

I'd been so wrong.

Tag would pay for this. I would make him pay

one way or another.

~

Present day...

I took the whole five minutes I asked for. One minute to pack my guns in my pockets and four minutes to reflect.

To reflect on the day when everything went to hell. It was the kind of situation that tore a person apart.

I'd wanted revenge. I'd wanted some form of justice to what had been done to me, and I surely got mine. Revenge was an evil thing that could go all sorts of ways.

You could take things into your hands and deal out justice, but it would come at a price.

It always did, and that price was something that could expand to an abysmal black hole and get bigger and bigger. Harder to contain. Harder to manage.

That's what happened to me.

I'd caught Eloise cheating, I'd changed up the plans to get the diamonds and got them well before Tag and his boys could get there, then I'd sent them on a wild goose chase to get them all caught.

I'd thought prison would have been the result. The shipment contained priceless art and artifacts. It would have been clear as day that they were in the act of stealing the shipment.

But Eloise didn't just leave the house that day. She went to the docks in an attempt to save Tag.

Tag retaliated to Agent Peterson and his men indeed, and she got caught in the crossfire. Not just her. Tag's boys too.

In one flash he lost it all.

His family, and her.

I lost her.

My plan to exact revenge had ruined everything and set off the chain of events that followed me right to this point where these crazy people had taken my daughter. The last precious thing I had left in this world.

The phone ringing on my desk cut into my thoughts. My five minutes were probably up, and normally, I wouldn't have answered it, but I did now because of the situation.

"Hello, old friend." It was Tag. How convenient.

"Why are you calling me?"

I wasn't going to waste time talking shit.

"Just checking in. I got word your boys made it out of the facility. I'm impressed."

"Really?" This was me bullshitting him. Truthfully, I knew from the way Luc had explained what went down that neither he nor Claudius would have made it out alive without Maurice and Amelia's friends.

"Yes, really. Shows they have some balls. Two guys against a pack. Next time, they won't be so lucky."

Something sparked in me. It was his comment. *Two guys against a pack.*

Meaning he didn't know about the cops and Maurice.

"Oh yeah. When is next time?" More testing. I wanted to see if we could really harness the element of surprise.

"I'm about to tell you. We meet at eight. Bring the diamonds."

We'd be there a lot sooner than fucking eight.

"Where?" I asked pointedly.

"Clever, clever. I'll tell you closer to the time. Sit tight till then."

Good, we had the element of something. A window of some opportunity. We could be at Peyton in three hours. That would take us to around four. If we went through the old section of the prison like Cora suggested, we could get into the facility and catch them by surprise.

As to what would happen after that, I didn't know. I didn't know how I'd fare, but that didn't matter.

The two women I loved more than life itself had told me they hated me.

Before Amelia got taken, she'd given me that look of hate again, and it crushed me. I didn't know how she felt or what they were doing to her. It was all my fault.

There was one thing I needed to know though. One thing I had to know, and this was the perfect opportunity.

"You haven't said yet. How did you figure it out?" I asked.

"Millicent."

Great, confirmation of what I'd feared.

"Right."

"But you knew that and didn't want to believe it, just like how you didn't want to believe that your marriage was over." He gave me a sinister laugh.

A knife straight to my heart. I'd bet he loved that my wife chose him over me.

The days that followed after I'd caught them together were awful. I'd imagined all sorts of things. What they must have talked about, what they must have done. All that they did.

There was a day in between when Eloise had said she was going shopping and was away for much longer than her usual time. When she got home that night, I saw the few things she'd bought and immediately suspected that she'd been with Tag. I'd kept quiet right up to the big day when shit went down.

"You're right, and I was a fool. A fool to believe that things like loyalty and trust meant anything. A fool to trust a wife I'd always been faithful to and believed she was faithful to me too. A fool to trust a friend or take a man like you for a friend when you would easily turn around and take the thing I loved the most. I was a fool to believe Millicent couldn't be turned against me. Yes, Tag. I know I did so much wrong, so much wrong in this whole thing, and the things that I'm sorry for are that you lost your boys and Eloise died. But, fuck, I still want you dead. I still have the same vendetta against you. So, I'm not sorry for setting you up. I'm not sorry for your pain. I'm not sorry for anything I did to you. I'm sorry for the results."

It was the end for me. It was the end of my road, the end of my journey, and it wouldn't matter what happened to me. I'd say whatever the hell I liked. Right now, I could because I still had something he wanted.

The diamonds.

I still had them, and he wanted them. So, fuck him. He'd hear the truth, alright, and I wasn't sorry for him. The only difference between years ago and now was that I wanted him dead more than ever. Back then, my goal had been prison for a long time. Long enough to get him out of the picture.

I was a fool to think that with him gone I could save my marriage. Even after seeing Eloise with him, I'd been willing to forgive her.

He was silent for a minute or so, and I grew more eager because we had to go. My question, however, hadn't been answered.

I knew he hadn't hung up because I could hear him breathing. He was probably seething from my words, but I didn't give a flying fuck.

"So, *old friend*." I emphasized the words. "How about we pick up where you left off in your explanation. You got to the part about Millicent."

"I came back to Chicago after spending years in Italy, hiding. Remember, you arranged for me to get gone."

I'd arranged that because the feds were after him and he was after Agent Peterson. If Tag had gotten to him, I knew Agent Peterson would have talked and Tag would have known everything. Without his boys and the state Tag was in that night, he was useless to himself. He'd called me straight after the whole craziness went down. He'd called me in tears over the lives that were lost. He was how I'd found out Eloise had been killed.

"I remember." His call had been followed by Agent Peterson's. I didn't know which call was worse. Tag giving me the initial blow or Agent Peterson telling me he'd accidentally shot my wife. She'd run right into his line of fire and got hit. It was an accident, but I didn't care. "Don't pussyfoot around the situation. Talk."

He laughed. "I wanted to come home. Italy isn't Chicago. I think though that most of all I wanted to see you. I should have found it weird that through all those years, we never stayed in touch. I left, couldn't even bury my boys properly and say goodbye to Eloise, and you never stayed in touch. It should have been a giveaway, but I foolishly thought it was for my protection. Calls can be traced."

"You're pussyfooting again." I didn't want to hear all the fluff about how he felt or what he thought. Much as it was a part of the story.

"I went to your house and saw Millicent. You

were away. She was shocked to see me, and it was what she said then that revealed all."

My heart gripped as suspense truly took me. This was it. The moment of reckoning.

"What did she say?"

"First, she looked confused to see me, and disgusted. I wondered why she looked like that." He chuckled. Millicent looked disgusted because the night I'd seen Eloise and Tag together, she'd been the one and only person I'd told. I was a grief-stricken man with a broken heart who needed to confide in someone. She was at home tucking Amelia into bed by the time I'd returned. "I thought she must not have recognized me. I stupidly reminded her who I was, but she knew me and said that she was surprised I would dare come here. The woman was defending you. You know, Raphael, she truly was a friend because that little woman didn't care who I was when she started her tirade. What she didn't know was that I never knew you knew about the affair."

Fuck, that was how it started. Wow. It was amazing.

"So, you figured it out from what she said?"

"Not exactly. It was what Eloise said right before your agent's bullet got her. I saw her running across the docks. When she saw me, she screamed 'He knows. Get out.'" He paused for a minute. "She said that, and I thought she meant someone else. I thought she was talking about the agent. *He knows.* I never put two and two together that *he* was you. She was trying to tell me that you knew about us and I was in the middle of a trap. Bullets were already being fired, and it got her just then. It wasn't until Millicent said she was amazed that you and I were still friends after what I did to your marriage that it came together in my mind. Then she all but confirmed it all in disgust when she said it was unforgiveable to betray you the way I did by having an affair with your wife."

I held my breath and released it slowly. "So, that's it."

"That's it. It took a few days to sink in. A few days to do a little more digging and realize that the feds didn't get the diamonds in the shipment, so you must have got to them first, and a few days to come up with my grand plan for you. Blood for blood. Your daughter for my sons and Eloise."

"You know that same daughter is hers too."

"She's yours, and Eloise is gone. It's enough. When I found out she'd left home, and damn, you took great lengths to cover her identity, that just encouraged me more."

"How did you then get Millicent to betray me?"

Last question, and then I was done.

"The same way I do everything else. Everyone has a price. Everyone has something they can be made to do if you threaten them enough. For her it was her husband. When I put it all together, I threatened to kill her husband if she didn't cooperate."

So, that was it.

Yes, that would indeed be Millicent's price. She loved her husband the way I'd wanted my wife to love me. She would have done anything to save him, even if it meant betraying me.

The way it had played out and from what I knew of Tag back then, I knew that if he'd gotten his hands on Agent Peterson, the man would have sung like a canary and told Tag it was me who'd put him up to the whole trap. Blood for blood.

I'd known Tag would have wanted Amelia. He'd lost his boys and Eloise, and he would have wanted her dead too.

To my poor girl, I'd run a successful business. She'd never known who I really was. It was part of my job to keep everything business related out of her life. My men hadn't even known I had a daughter. Just Tag and Marcus. That was it, and even then, I hadn't allowed any association for safety reasons.

No one had to tell me that Tag would have sought revenge on me by getting to Amelia. I'd known he would kill her because he would have wanted me to feel the same pain he felt. I knew how his mind worked. I'd never expected Amelia to leave home the way she did and for any of what happened to happen. It hadn't been in the cards. So, my mission had been to keep her even more secret.

Now was the time of reckoning. All the secrets were jumping straight out of the closet. Right into the open for all to see.

Luc came into the office with a frown on his face, probably checking to see what the holdup was with me.

It was time to go.

"Eight o'clock, Tag." I looked at Luc as I spoke, and his eyes widened when he realized who I was speaking to. "This ends today."

"You bet." Tag hung up, and I placed the phone back on the hook.

"That was Tag?" Luc asked, moving closer.

"It was, and they don't know about the cops. He wants to meet at eight. We have an advantage and a window."

"Let's go." He nodded firmly.

One thing I'd admired about this guy since his

return to Chicago was his love for my daughter.

She was his price. No one had to tell me that he would do anything for her.

It was evident in everything he did.

He turned to go, but I stopped him. I took off my family ring and held it out to him.

"Your ring. Why are you giving me that?" He furrowed his brows.

"Whoever wears it owns the business."

He shook his head at me. "Raphael, I'm honored, but like I told you, I don't want it. If we make it, I'm taking Amelia out of this life."

I rested my hand on his shoulder and smiled. "That's why you should have it. It was always yours. You take it and give it to whomever you see fit."

He looked at the ring, staring at it for a few moments before he took it. "Thank you… I'll make sure who gets it will definitely be fit for the job."

I gave him a curt nod. "Let's go."

Time for showdown. Time to face my enemies. And if I died, it would be time to face death.

I'd finished the Bible last night.

In my state of sorrow, I took to it.

At the end, the conclusion I'd come to was, it wouldn't matter what I did. There was no place in heaven for a devil like me.

CHAPTER 14

Amelia

That was it.

About an hour ago, I'd managed to loosen the tension around my thumb and forefinger on my left hand. These ropes were bound so tightly that it was perhaps pointless to think I could break free, but I would try.

My goal was to try. To try for Gigi.

She'd been shuffling around, moving her head from side to side occasionally, although she wasn't awake.

It was like she was stuck in a dream, or rather, in our case, a nightmare.

When my fingers had come free, I'd wiggled them and tried to feel for a knot. I knew if I could get one knot loose, then maybe the tension would break on the rest.

I'd spent the last hour trying to do that, and just now, a little section gave way, so I could slip my finger through the hook. God, all this with my hands tied behind my back. I had to visualize what I was doing while trying not to make it look obvious.

I was certain that there were cameras in here. It would have been foolish if this room wasn't under surveillance.

I couldn't see anything around me, and I couldn't see what was behind me because of the way I was positioned.

Footsteps echoed along the wooden floor, and a hideous man approached the barred door to the cell.

I'd taken to thinking of this as a cell because of the setup and the fact that we were here tied up, waiting to die.

The man who opened the door looked like a cross between a toad and a lizard. He was bald, bulky, and had terrible teeth. Yellow and brown in appearance.

He smiled, showing off the display, and looked me over.

"Just checking on you two dolls."

I wouldn't talk to him. I didn't need to. This was a lackey, a grunt as far as I was concerned.

"I get to play with this one later." He pointed at Gigi, and I narrowed my eyes.

His smile grew, and he walked over to her. I winced as he raised his hand and slapped her across her face.

"Stop it!" I yelled.

The slap to Gigi's face woke her up, and she cried out and looked around her fiercely with tears running from her eyes.

The man laughed. "I knew that would get some reaction from you. I followed you in LA. Followed the two of you."

I held his gaze. I didn't remember seeing him.

"I was there at the ballet watching you and that oaf. I was the biker, as they called me."

"Leave me alone."

"For now. Maybe I'll have what's left of you when Victor's done." He licked his lips and looked from me to Gigi, then left us.

I watched him until he walked down the length of the bars and disappeared.

We had to get out of here.

I had to get Gigi out of here. She was my friend and didn't deserve to be part of any of this.

I looked to her, and my heart ached.

"Gigi," I cried.

"Amelia, I'm in so much pain." Her lips were so swollen she could barely talk.

"What did they do to you?" I had to know. All manner of things had flooded my mind as to what she could have gone through.

"Electrocuted me, tortured me. It was awful. I couldn't stop screaming from the pain."

"God, Gigi, I'm so sorry." My heart squeezed.

She winced and shook her head. I thought she was going to tell me that she wanted nothing to do with me, and I would have understood. It was perfectly understandable for her to want that.

She could be dead right now.

"If we get out of this, I will personally vet every single friend you have, and for fuck's sake, I think you need to either work in a different department or choose another career." She actually laughed.

I couldn't believe she was laughing. But that was Gigi. It was what she did when she knew a situation looked bad. Granted, this had never happened to us before, but she was being herself.

"I'm so sorry this happened to you. I'm so sorry, and I understand if you hate me." I thought I should be the one to say it.

"No. No, Amelia, don't you dare say that to me. Don't you dare. I know this isn't you. It's these guys."

"I'm going to get you out of here," I promised.

"How?" Through her bruises, I could see the look of confusion on her face.

"My fingers are loose. I think I may be able to do something." I didn't want to say any more just in case I could be heard, and I certainly wouldn't talk about the key.

"God, Amelia, try. I can't from here. Rope's too tight, and even if I wanted to, I wouldn't be able to break free. I'm too weak."

"Don't worry. I'm trying."

It was all about trying to relax and focus. Visualize the movements just like I would if I were dancing. Seeing the move before it happened. Seeing it all before it happened and working with that.

In my mind's eye I saw the knot and moved my finger. Slowly and up, and up. Then across to where the bulk of the knot was and where it twisted.

Oh God, my finger moved in and shifted it out. Oh God...

I can do this. I think I did it.

I did. The hold actually loosened, and the tackle it had on the other knots loosened too.

"Gigi, I need you to stay calm and work with me. Is there a camera behind me?" I needed to know before I shook the ropes off. If there was a camera—and I suspected there was—then I'd probably only have a matter of minutes to get the key, free Gigi, and get out of here. Exactly in that order.

I didn't know where Victor and the men were stationed. It didn't seem like they'd come from far.

"There's a camera, Amelia. It's just above your head."

"Okay. I need you to focus on running when the time comes. Just that. Just use whatever strength you have left and focus on running. When we get outside, I don't want you to think of me or anything else. I need you to think of you."

"Amelia." She winced, and her eyes were full of worry. "I can't do that."

"Gigi, please, this is life or death. It literally is.

The fact of the matter is, you're probably being kept alive for some purpose."

She gasped on hearing that.

"You think so?"

"Yes," I replied with certainty.

I was certain the purpose would be more than just to be used as some damn toy. They would use her in some way. Just like they'd used her to lure Luc and the others away. The strongest men had left, which had opened the doors for Tag to take me. It wasn't even that hard. Everyone had prepped for battle, but all it took was Millicent.

Put someone I trusted completely in front of my face, and my guard dropped.

I still couldn't believe this was her. I would never have guessed she'd be a threat.

It was all so obvious now though that it was her. I just didn't want to believe it. Another person who broke my trust. *Mom, Dad, Luc, Millicent.*

It was funny they all loved me and had good intentions, but it wasn't enough.

I shook my head. It wasn't time to think about any of that.

Focus.

Focusing was the key. It was the key to hopefully saving my friend.

"Now, Gigi. Now. Ready?"

She sucked in a sharp breath and nodded.

Okay, well, here I go. This was the epitome of all my years of being a cop.

If it was only for this one moment. To save her.

I slipped the ropes from my hands and methodically bent down to undo the ropes from my legs.

Visualization. I had it all figured out, and so far, it was working.

I grabbed the key and made my way to Gigi.

Hands first, then I undid the rope binding her feet. My hands were working like magic, undoing the knots as quickly as I could.

As Gigi stood, I moved to the lock on the door hoping like hell Millicent hadn't screwed me over and this wasn't some stupid game to make us think we could escape when we couldn't.

I could have cried when the lock clicked open and the door moved out.

Oh God, we could do this.

Gigi was behind me. We walked out to the corridor. I looked in the opposite direction to where everyone else had gone. There was a path that turned.

"This way. Run as fast as you can." I pointed down the passage, and we started running.

Jesus Christ, off in the distance, behind us, I could hear hurried footsteps.

They must have seen us on camera.

I ran for all I was worth, and thankfully, Gigi was keeping up with me.

We turned down the corridor, and it was darker. No light but ounces of daylight shone through in various cracks under the doors and around the windows we passed. This section looked old. Old and completely out of use.

We ran into a large hall that held benches and tables. A cafeteria long out of use.

This place really was a prison. I could see all the cells now, overhead and all around. So, I was going to guess that this was the only abandoned prison I knew of, and it wasn't in Chicago. If I managed to get to a phone or find some way of contacting Luc, I'd at least be able to tell him where I was.

We turned down another corridor. This one was much darker. I took Gigi's hand when she started to slow down. Ahead was a brighter light, so we ran toward it.

Go toward the light?

Yes, indeed.

There was a room off to the corner that you could easily miss. There. That might be a good hiding spot. Just somewhere we could come up with a plan.

The darkness gave us cover.

I was sure we could still be seen if they looked hard, but darkness made it possible for us to hide.

We went into the room and locked the door. In true old-school style, it had a bolt from the inside, and a lock.

The only light came from the window, and it was one of those windows that couldn't be opened. It wasn't surprising given the nature of the place we were in. And this room...

There was a metal chair that looked like something from one of the classic Frankenstein films.

It had metal manacles on the arms and a helmet-looking dome-shaped device that hovered above it.

"Amelia, I think it's safe to say we're at Peyton Prison." Gigi looked nervously around the room.

Peyton Prison, yes I remembered seeing this place on TV. "Yeah, looks that way."

"You know this was a heavily secured psychiatric unit?"

I didn't know that part. "No, but look at the chair."

She walked over to a cupboard and opened it.

Inside were some bottles with the poison warning tags on it.

"Hydrogen peroxide," she said and looked around some more. "Lots of it, and bleach. Amelia, I could make a potion with this."

Oh Jesus. "Gigi, for God's sake, this is not the time for that." Maybe she hit her head.

She rolled her eyes at me. "I mean, I can make a bomb."

"God, really?" A bomb could and would be very useful.

"Look around the room for stuff we can use. I need something to mix the stuff in. A bowl or something like that."

More focusing.

I jumped into action and started looking. When I went to the cupboard by the window, I noticed for the first time how high up we were. I would say maybe the fifth floor. It had felt more like we'd been on the ground floor with the cafeteria, but again, it made sense for everything to be so high up. Plus, there was probably more than one cafeteria in this place.

The prison was massive.

I opened another cupboard and saw it was one of those pulley elevators. The kind you might put mail in from the ground floor and pull it up. I looked into the shaft, inspecting it. Looked sturdy enough. This could be our escape route. Outside, I could see the river. There had to be an exit from this side of the building.

"I found a bowl and some kerosene. That will help with the reaction."

"Great." I nodded and opened another closet. There were a few empty medicine bottles in there.

I grabbed those and went to the little table where she'd set everything up.

"Will this help?"

"Perfect. I'll pour the liquid in, and we can have a couple each. All you need to do is drop it as hard as you can. When the glass smashes, it will blow up and release a gas that will sting their eyes."

"How do you know all this?"

"Chemistry. I did advanced Chem in high school. I loved it, even though I loved art more. It felt like mixing potions to me." She chuckled.

It was so like her to say that. My friend was a brilliant artist but also a practicing witch. I would be the first one to roll my eyes at her sayings, predictions, and ideas, but I was thanking my lucky stars now.

She mixed away from an assortment of bottles.

Looked like she'd found more than what she'd mentioned before.

I held my breath, feeling the tension. It was too quiet, and I didn't know when we'd get found.

We'd heard footsteps when we first broke out of the cell, and the guys must have known there was only one way we could have gone.

Gigi started pouring the mixture into the bottles I'd found.

She got to the sixth one when we heard voices. Then footsteps.

"Shit," I hissed.

Gigi poured the mixture into two more bottles. Making that eight. There were two more, but we didn't have enough mixture.

"This will have to do," she whispered.

I nodded. "Gigi, here." I gave her six bottles and kept two for myself as an idea formed in my head.

"No, we should get four each," she protested.

I placed my hand over my lips and signaled for her to be quiet. There was someone walking by the door.

While she stood still, I placed the bottles in her pocket and nodded.

"Search every room," called a voice from the

other side of the door. It sounded like the biker. Ugh, I would hate for him to find us.

"I'm looking," replied another guy. "It's hard to see with no camera and power on this side."

No cameras and no power. That was good. My skin tingled, and I released a slow sigh.

They walked away from the door, and I grabbed Gigi's hands.

I practically shoved her in the elevator shaft.

"What are you doing?" Gigi hissed.

"Please remember what I said. Focus on you. When this gets to wherever it leads to, hide. Please." I gave her a nod of conviction.

"We can escape together," she insisted with wide, frightened eyes.

"It's better this way. I get to make sure you make it out this way. I can't risk them coming in here and seeing where you went."

"Pleas—"

"Gigi, please, we're running out of time."

"Okay... you better be safe, Amelia. You're my sister. Who else will I eat a whole Bangkok street feast and burgers with?" She went to hug me, but the door handle started turning.

"Door's locked from inside," the guy called out.

"Shoot it down." The biker bellowed.

I didn't waste another minute. I closed the

gate, locking Gigi in. She took hold of the rope pulley on the inside and started wheeling herself down.

As she went down, her eyes never left mine. Her tear-filled eyes never left mine.

She was my sister too. I hoped she knew how much I loved her.

Blessed be Gigi.

A gunshot sounded against the door, making me jump.

When another fired, I closed the closet, sealing off the elevator. Hopefully protecting Gigi.

This was it. I had nowhere to run. Nowhere to hide.

The only weapons I had were these two little bottles of Gigi's potion.

Focus, concentrate.

Focus.

Another shot sent the door flying open, and biker guy smiled when he saw me.

CHAPTER 15

Luc

~

I damn well hated to admit, it but if Maurice hadn't brought Max, Sinclaire, and Cora with him to Chicago, we would have been screwed.

Screwed with no hope, screwed and running around like headless chickens, not knowing what the hell to do.

We would have been well and truly fucked and just damn players in a sick game designed by psychos.

Yesterday, I hadn't thought I had much hope left, and hell, I still probably didn't, but what we had now that we didn't have yesterday was opportunity.

Opportunity and tact.

Cora had worked some damn magic and was able to give us a map to plan out everything.

The plan was to get inside the prison via the sewer that would lead straight into the building. It would take us to the back side, where there was no power. It was the side that had housed the more-acute-level prisoners.

She'd set out all the areas that had surveillance, and this way was the best. We could get inside without being seen.

We were in the sewer now and had just walked two miles in from the park.

The place was empty and as abandoned as most of everything on this side.

We weren't far now.

That was what I kept telling myself, so I could keep my focus.

Not long now. Not far now.

And again, it was all hands on deck.

There were twenty of us, and we'd left fifty more guys who would get to the prison above ground. They were scheduled to get there just after us. The second wave of our army made up of a combo of our guys and our alliances.

We were going in guns blazing.

It made me feel uncomfortable though that Raphael was here. He shouldn't have come.

We trekked through the passage proceeding along the length. Just behind me, I could hear Sinclaire and Max whispering, but I couldn't' hear what they were saying.

Couldn't have been anything good if they were talking about me.

Raphael and Pa were at the back of the line. I'd asked Pa to keep an eye on Raphael.

The two were the weakest of our pack, so it was best for them to stay out of the way.

Claudius pushed his way up to me and nudged my shoulder.

"You cool?" He nodded to me.

"As ever." I leaned closer, so the others couldn't hear me. "Claudius, as soon as we see the girls, give them to Pa and Raphael and tell them to get the hell out of here."

"Absolutely. Raphael's struggling to keep up."

We both glanced behind us and saw that he'd stopped and Pa was talking to him.

Fuck, if he died down here, I'd never forgive myself. I should have insisted more on him staying behind. I understood why he'd come, but damn.

"Don't worry. We got this." I didn't know how

Claudius could sound so positive, but I appreciated it.

"You better hope we got this," Sinclaire cut in.

Claudius and I both looked at him.

"Or else what, cop boy?" Claudius glared.

Sinclaire narrowed his eyes and said nothing.

"That's what I thought." Claudius stopped walking. "Do me a favor and stop pissing me off. My brother is an angel compared to me. I won't think twice about cutting your face off and wearing it as a hat."

Maurice laughed, and Claudius glared at him, stopping his laugher instantly.

"Come on, guys, now's not the time," Max offered and gave Sinclaire a hard look.

I didn't say anything. I just kept walking. I didn't care about Sinclaire or whatever shit he had to say.

He could continue talking out of his ass, for all I cared. It was water on a duck's back.

We weren't far.

Twenty minutes later proved me right. The tunnel went on, but we were right at the spot that would lead to the ground floor toilets. Above us was a large metal drain cover with the words *Peyton Prison* engraved in it.

Claudius and The Four got their tools out and

got to work on unscrewing the bolts that held the cover in place.

It took a little bit longer than anticipated because of the rust that had formed around the bolts, but they did it.

Next order of business was going up.

Claudius and I helped everyone get inside and left ourselves for last.

He got me in, then I pulled him inside.

Sure enough, we were indeed in the toilets. The toilets that smelled stale like old piss and mold mixed together. Although the place was dark, daylight that snuck in from the frosted glass windows showed enough. Cobwebs cascaded over the ceiling, and the floor was covered in dirt and dust.

It was so dusty that the particles wafted off the ground in clouds as we moved.

I guess as bad as the place looked and smelled, it showed one thing.

No one had been down here in a very long time.

"What now?" Max asked me.

"Amelia and Gigi are on the fifth floor. We can get to the cell she's in from this side. The surveillance stops just beyond the corridor she's being kept, so we have to be ready to party when we come up on camera." At least it would be a lot of us. The strongest team.

"Okay. Let's do this."

We moved through the toilet and went out to the corridor which kept that dank smell about it. Dank and mold. It instantly made me feel like taking a bath.

The place reeked of uncleanliness, but more than dirt. It was the evil done by the prisoners that had been held here and died here. This place was one of the facilities that conducted the death penalty by both poison and electrocution. They did other things too, of the inhumane variety.

Lobotomies and other things I didn't want to save in my brain.

It was typical Victor style. I was sure he'd come up with the idea to use this place. Somewhere undetected and off radar. We wouldn't have thought to look here because it wasn't even in Chicago. We were in Pent Water Michigan. Well outside of our realms.

Something grabbed my attention when we got to the corridor with the steps leading to the first floor.

It was a shuffling noise. Could have been a rat, but I was sure I heard a whimper.

Maurice inched over. "Boss, you hear that?"

"I heard something." I held my hand up for everyone to stop.

Raphael looked at me. "What why are we stopping?"

"Shhh."

I cocked my head to Maurice, signaling for him and Saul to follow.

The noise came from that cupboard by the reception area. Looked like a coat closet.

I grabbed the handle and flung the door open. Someone ran out, bolted out more like, and ran straight past me. They looked back and held up their hand high but froze.

I could have cried tears of joy as I looked at Gigi. She was so covered in dirt and dust I could hardly see her face, and her hair was covered too.

"Luc!" she cried and came hurtling back, throwing herself into my arms.

I hugged her hard. "Gigi, God in heaven."

"I can't believe you're here." She shook and started crying.

When she eventually pulled away, Maurice took her.

"Doll." His voice sounded so emotional I couldn't believe it was him.

"I thought you died." Gigi cupped his face and pressed a kiss to his lips.

"Nah, I'm like a cat. Got at least seven more lives left in me."

Max and Sinclaire looked on, watching her. I wondered what they must have thought. Gigi was the nicest person ever, and here she was, fraternizing with mobsters.

When she saw them, she rushed to them too. "You guys. You—" Her voice trailed off when she looked over and saw Raphael.

These past days, I'd seen many sides to this man.

This side was the father who just wanted to get his daughter back.

In his eyes, Amelia was still his child. I understood completely. Gigi walked toward him, looking him over.

"You're Amelia's dad," she observed.

"I am." Raphael could barely talk.

"Your eyes. They're just like hers."

He nodded. "Where is she, Gigi?"

The look of angst on Gigi's face caught and gripped me. I moved closer to hear her.

"She's still up there on the fifth floor. We managed to escape the cell and hide, but she's still up there. She sent me down here in a lift shaft. She was in an old medical room. They... came in after her. I wanted to stay and fight, but she made me go."

"Fuck," I breathed and covered my mouth. It was typical Amelia. I would have done the same thing. Sacrifice my safety to protect my loved ones.

Gigi turned back to me. "Luc, please, you have to get to her. You have to save her. Knight of cups." She nodded.

She'd called me that once after I'd picked up one of her tarot cards with the image of a knight carrying a cup. I wished that I could have appreciated the reference, but I couldn't. I wasn't that person. I wasn't there for Amelia when she needed me. She got taken, and now we were here in this mess.

"I will get her back, even if it kills me." Time to shake things up a bit. "Pa... come here." Dad came closer. "Gigi, this is my father. He's going to get you some place safe. Amelia's father will go with you too—"

Just as I thought, dear old Raphael cut in. "I'm going with you. I told you. You can't send me back." He squared his shoulders and gave me daggers.

"Like fuck. Of course, I'm sending you back."

"Luc, I will kill you here."

"Raphael," Pa snapped and moved closer.

"You're going to slow them down. Look at you, you can't even breathe properly. Listen for a fucking change."

"No. I'm going," the stubborn old fool said. "You can't tell me what to do."

I pulled out the ring he'd given me earlier and shoved it on my hand, then waved it in front of his face.

"I think you'll find that I can. I'm in charge here, and I'm pulling rank. Don't cross me, or I will kill you." I bared my teeth and stared him down.

Max stepped in, literally stepped in front of Raphael and me.

"Hey, we don't have time for this shit," He held up his hands and whirled around to face Raphael. "With every due respect, Mr. Rossi, I think Luc's right."

"I can't just leave." Raphael frowned.

"Okay, how about you stay here with some of your guys and watch surveillance. I think we should split up anyway. This is how we'd lead a team on a raid. Can we do that?"

I had to give the guy credit for his attempt.

I nodded, agreeing. "You four," I pointed to the four guys in the back. "Stay with the boss." I called Raphael *boss* out of habit.

They nodded, agreeing.

"Keep watch, and by God, Raphael, if you see Amelia come this way, you take her and go. You hear me? Take her out of here and go. Don't be some hero and go after Tag. Leave that part to us."

"Sure," Raphael finally agreed. "*Boss.*"

It threw me off kilter to hear him call me that. It didn't have the effect I thought it would. The effect I'd dreamed of so long ago. Because I'd changed so much.

I gave him a curt nod.

"Okay, let's do this." I walked on ahead and looked back at Raphael. He continued to watch me. That look was still in his eyes. I knew how badly he must have wanted to join us, but this had gone long past sympathy or empathy.

Those things were weaknesses on a battlefield. They would be weaknesses in Victor's arena.

CHAPTER 16

Amelia

Punch.

Kick... upper cut. Kick, punch. Kick.

I got him. The tallest guy. I sent a kick straight to his sternum and pushed up his neck. Something snapped, and he fell backwards.

One down, and another just came to take his place.

I'd been waiting for the right moment to use the bombs. I needed an opening, so I could get to the door first, but the guys were in the way. Now more.

There were six of them now, and I got the impression that they were playing with me. Toying with me and loving the fact that it was me against them.

Sure, I could give as good as I got, but there was a limit. I had a limit, and I'd gone past it. I was getting tired, and they were too strong for me.

Out of my league. *Above me,* as Luc would have said.

He would have been right.

Two of them rushed at me, giving me a small opening to get to the door. I leapt into the air as they were about to grab me and sent a flying kick to the closest guy. It took him out.

Now. Now was my chance. I ran to the door, twisted back on myself, and threw the bombs. Both of them.

Biker guy ducked for cover behind the chair. The others weren't so lucky. The minute the bottles hit the floor, they exploded. Shards of glass sparked from it, piercing in their skin, but it was the chemical reaction that packed the punch. The liquid hit the floor, then blew up.

It shocked me, and again, I thanked my lucky stars for Gigi. I didn't know she knew how to do stuff like that. God.

I turned to run, feeling hopeful that I just

might make it, but damn it, not paces away from me stood ten more guys. They all came at me, and we started fighting. Again.

I fought with all the energy in my being, but there were too many of them.

"Give up, girlie. Great show and good fight," biker guy taunted. He coughed as he came out of the room.

One of the guys landed a fist in my jaw, and I staggered backwards seeing stars floating before me.

I thought I was going to collapse from the impact. My stomach felt queasy again, and it was all I could do not to keel over and vomit.

I moved away, still trying to break away from them, but two of them grabbed me before I could even pull in a breath.

They ushered me to biker guy, who'd been watching me fight off his goons. The smile on his face grew wider and turned into a laugh.

A very haughty, satisfied laugh that sent shivers down my spine. I kicked out at him, using the guys holding me up for balance.

Biker guy, however, was quicker than I expected, and sharper than he looked. He bared those disgusting teeth to me as he grabbed my leg and stabbed my thigh with something sharp.

I screamed. The thing pierced through my skin and felt like a needle. It was a needle, a syringe with a big needle on the end, and shit...

No...

My leg... I couldn't feel it.

When he dropped my leg, it dangled with no life, and I couldn't move it.

"What did you do to me!" I screamed.

"Just a little something to calm you down. A general anesthetic, if you will. This paralyses you, so we can torture you with ease." He laughed. "Come on, boys."

I tried to break free of their hold on me to no avail. Even if I did manage to free myself, where would I run? My leg...

Not feeling it was the strangest sensation ever.

It was awful, just awful.

What was worse was being taken back to where I'd run from. The cell. But we didn't go inside. They walked me past it and into another room. It looked like a waiting area. Tag sat on a sofa and stood as we came in. Victor came through the door on the opposite side of the room and started hollering with such deep laughter there was no doubt he was crazy. Completely and utterly crazy.

"Amelia," Tag hissed. "I am not amused by your little stunt."

"I didn't do it to a amuse you, so fuck you."

The guy holding me the tightest tightened his grip even more.

"Really?"

"Fucking asshole, let me go. Let me go!"

I didn't care that I might have sounded just as crazy as Victor. This was the end, and I didn't care.

"Victor, go get the other one," Tag said.

"No!" I wailed.

He ignored me and continued speaking to Victor. "Kill her ass. She's served her purpose. Was going to use her a little more, but I'm accelerating things. No need to keep pets when you don't have room. Here, there is no room for insolence. She couldn't have gotten far."

"Leave her out of this. She has nothing to do with you."

Tag just looked at me. "I don't care. She's linked to you, and you are linked to Raphael. Plus, she knows where we are. That's bad. *Real bad*. Now… the question on my mind is this: How'd you escape so easily?"

"Fuck you," I screamed.

"That's not an answer."

I pushed back against the guys holding me and kicked out with my good leg like some wild, feral creature.

Like before, my leg was grabbed, and Tag plunged another needle in.

This time, the paralysis came quickly. Before I could get over the numbness, he stabbed me in my right arm.

I cried out from the pain.

Tag laughed, and the men set me down on the ground.

"You know, I just thought of something." He put his forefinger to his temple.

"Raphael thinks you're alive. He has the diamonds, and he'll be here by eight with them. As long as he thinks you're alive, that's all that matters. You don't have to be alive anymore."

I started shaking when he pulled out his gun. I would never beg for my life. That was the last thing that would sink me to the abysmal black hole my life had become.

I had happy moments though. Happy moments with Luc.

I actually fell in love. It didn't matter who he was or what he was. He loved me.

I hoped he knew that I'd always loved him.

He'd saved me right from day one. But the biggest thing he'd saved was my heart. I'd found myself because of him. And now I would die.

I love you, Luc...

I watched Tag raise his gun. Adjust it in line with my head and pull the trigger back. He released it, and I waited to welcome the bullet straight into my head.

Will it hurt, or will I die instantly?

I'd never know because someone shoved me out of the way...

Someone shoved me hard, and I rolled over onto my side. A scream of terrifying anguish echoed through the room. I flopped over to see Millicent grabbing her chest and screaming. Wailing in agony.

The bullet...

It hit her... it hit her in her chest. It hit her.

She took it for me.

Saved me.

"Nooooo!" I screamed.

Blood spurted from her lips.

I tried to move. It was so hard with just one arm, but I moved to her, pulling and sliding until I got to her. Tag started to laugh.

"Millicent. No..."

"Amelia, I'm sorry." Her voice was just above a

whisper. Soft and searching. Barely there. Blood covered the whole front of her pink cardigan.

"Stay with me," I begged.

"It's my fault. All my fault. I didn't mean to. I didn't mean to. They were going to kill my husband. I love you, sweet girl."

I watched the light and the life leave her eyes. It literally was like someone had switched something off. Something deep inside her.

I screamed and tried to wake her, but nothing. "No, oh God. No. Please."

Millicent...

She'd been so dear to me. Always. In my mind I could see her with me as a child. She'd always been there. From as far back as I could remember. With her milk and cookies taking care of me.

She'd been there when I'd brought home my first leotard, there to pick me up when I felt down. She'd cleaned up all the things I broke in the house as I practiced my moves, and covered for me because my parents didn't like me prancing around the place for that very reason. She'd been the only person I'd told about the first guy I crushed on, and my first kiss. My parents would have gone apeshit at me, and things like that had best been reserved for Millicent.

She'd been there when the letter came from

Julliard, accepting me. It had been the two of us who were the first to know and celebrate.

She'd been like a mother to me.

Now she was gone.

"Pity, pity. I really wanted her to see me kill her husband. It's no fun now that she's dead. You people are so fickle. I can almost guess your price. Haven't you heard about guarding your secrets with your life? Or rather your weaknesses. With her, all I did was threaten to kill her husband. That was her price, and look where it got her. Never did like her though. Always, she stuck her nose where it didn't belong. Damn nosy bitch."

"You bastard! Why did you drag her into this mess?" I could barely see him through my tears.

"Dear old Millicent here was the one who gave the game away. She was the rat, the person who started this whole show. She notified me of your father's knowledge of my affair with your mother, and from that, I realized what happened years ago. Your father set me up. He's to blame for why you don't have a mother and, of course, your current predicament."

"You take no blame, none whatsoever. You had an affair with your best friend's wife. That is the cause of all of this. Youuuuuuu!" I bellowed.

His face flushed red, and he rushed to me with the gun and pressed it to my head.

"Don't you speak to me like that." He snarled, nostrils flaring and eyes blazing.

"Kill me. Go ahead. I don't care. Just know this. It was your fault. All of it. All of this. You, the disloyal friend who broke a family apart. Things could have been different. My mother would be here if not for you."

I swore he was about to pull the trigger again, but he stopped when one of his lackeys burst into the room.

"Boss, Dino said he saw one of Raphael's men on the second floor." The guy blurted in a hurried babble.

Tag straightened up in fury and growled. "What!"

I looked at the guy. He was scraggly looking with a scar on his chin. If one of Dad's men was here, then that meant Luc was here.

My heart squeezed at the prospect. I didn't think he would have been able to find me. I didn't know how he had.

"That's fine. Go after them," Tag ordered. "I don't know how your people found us, but they'll pay. Let's change things up and take this to the roof. I'll bet you'll look just like an angel hanging from it."

Oh God...

CHAPTER 17

Luc

~

"Luc, stop." Claudius grabbed my arm and pulled me close to him. He pointed up to the floor above us.

We were in the atrium that ran across to the other side of the building. According to the map, it would take us up to the section we wanted to get to the fifth floor.

I looked up and saw three figures coming at us fast.

Fuck. I thought this might happen because the guys would have gone after Amelia and Gigi, and they were still looking for Gigi. It made sense that they'd come this way.

"Time to change things up, boys," I called out.

Sinclaire flashed me a dark look and readied his gun.

"I'll grab a spot high up. It'll be useful." Max pulled out his rifle.

I liked his way of thinking.

"I'll watch your back," Sinclaire added. I doubted he would have wanted to stay without Max.

They left us and moved up the set of stairs leading to the left. It went up to a tower.

"Let's move, boys. Let's draw them this way," I ordered, and my men followed me into the hall to the right. I wasn't sure what this place could have been. Maybe a break room of sorts judging by the space it had. However, it reminded me of my high school auditorium.

I hated it, and I hated this place too.

High school was always a reminder of how poor we'd been back in LA, and how miserable life was. Hopelessness and, to some extent, helplessness.

Just like now.

"Where to, boss?" Maurice asked.

"Spread out. They saw us come in here."

"You heard the man." Dante smiled, pulling out his favorite guns. Two Berettas with the Japanese symbol for earth engraved on the handle.

"Dante, you take the lead," Claudius ordered. Dante gave him an odd look.

"And you?" he asked.

"Just do it." Dante cocked his head to the left, and Gio, Jude, and Alex followed. They went behind a wall that curved down to another corridor.

"Let's do this." Claudius slapped a hand on my back. "Boss."

"Yes, let's. Maurice and Saul, take the corner. Let's eliminate as much of them as we can." I ordered.

Footsteps sounded now, echoing on the concrete.

We moved. Claudius followed me, but we weren't going to take cover.

He knew what I meant to do without me having to say it.

"Luc, if I die—"

"Don't you fucking dare," I cut him off. "I need you. If I die, I need—"

"Lucian, don't you fucking dare. If you die, I will kill you myself."

Three goons ran through the door. Claudius and I ended them before they could get fully in. That warned the rest of the guys coming, and bullets sprayed in when they rushed in, coming at us from all directions. Just like at the facility, men came in, rushing in by the droves.

Like a plague.

Ten came. The bullets from The Four took them down, but they were replaced by more guys. Five got to us, and we started fighting.

A bullet from above took down the guy I was kicking.

That came from Max. He sent another bullet from his rifle straight to the head of the guy who was about to shoot Claudius.

More guys came. Fuck, there were so many of them.

Too many. Far too many.

The Four came out fighting and shooting, as did Maurice and Saul. It literally was like war.

Someone grabbed me, and I whirled around to face them. It was Claudius.

"Go!" he yelled. "Go find Amelia. We got this. You need to go."

I didn't want to leave him, but he was right. I should go. I realized this could be the last time I saw him. Our lighthearted jokes earlier aside.

I took the ring Raphael gave me off and handed it to him.

He looked at it, then back to me.

"The business is yours, just like I said." I told him.

"I'll clean it up," Claudius promised with a nod.

That surprised the shit out of me, but I didn't have time to be shocked.

I turned and rushed away, not looking back.

Best not to. Better to face what was ahead of me than look back.

I got to another set of stairs that led to the top, to where I needed to be. To Amelia. God, I hoped she was okay.

I ran up the stairs and turned. That was when I got hit with a sink.

The fucking thing came from nowhere and hit me so hard it knocked me back, sending me back down the steps I'd come.

Shit, my back... it felt broken. Cracked. I didn't know what the fuck.

The fall winded me, and the pain that rushed through my back nearly made me black out.

I blinked several times and took some deep breaths.

A bullet landed straight in my shoulder, making me scream.

"Fuck."

"Got ya," cooed Victor's voice in that sing-song fashion that irritated me to the core. Then the fucking bastard practically jumped from the ledge he was on and flew down toward me. He carried a sword. Some katana-looking thing that was so sharp it glinted with a sparkle. The lighting from the windows was poor, but I could see that if that thing got me, it would be the end of me.

I rolled out the way and pushed the pain out of my mind. Pushed it right out.

He stood and held it gracefully in the air.

"You know, in Russia, I got the chance to learn sword fighting. Samurai style. This is Shi Shi Mushi. The Japanese believe in naming their swords. Some for their deeds, some for their strengths. I gave it that name because of how I embued it."

"I couldn't give a flying fuck what you call your sword. Where's my girl?" I pulled out my gun and pointed it at him.

"Luc, you got here too early. She's not ready to see you yet. I mean, come on, dude. Raphael must have told you we'd contact you and give you the directions to get here for eight. When you think about it, the same result would have been achieved. Right?" He waved the sword around as he spoke.

"You know what? I'm bored now." I fired a shot at him, but he was quick. He dodged it. Then I did something I didn't normally do. I underestimated him.

I didn't think, and since we'd never actually fought like this, I'd never been able to assess his fighting skills.

Victor launched himself into the air with the grace of a dancer and the sharpness of a sword fighter. He whipped the sword across me and knocked the gun out of my hand.

I reached for my other gun, but he sent a roundhouse kick straight to my chest and knocked me flying.

Back on the ground, I winced and got up quickly. Victor looked scrawny and like he couldn't do much in a fight, but that was his advantage. He clearly had skill.

"So, I should let you know that I embued my beloved swords with viper venom. One nick, and you're dead. D.E.A.D. Ha ha ha."

Fuck. This just kept getting better and better.

This guy was a prick and a fucking half. He smiled on seeing my temporary stupor. I was going to have to really focus. A bullet in my arm didn't exactly help.

He came at me, but I dodged him. One more time, and I rolled to the left, closer to where I'd dropped my gun. No way was he just going to allow me to get it though.

The ferocious look on his face told me so.

I moved swiftly, fast, quickly, dodging his blows.

Swerving around him, I managed to land a kick in his back, sending him down to his knees. I took the opportunity to kick him down the stairs, and he dropped the sword.

Good, finally.

I launched myself down at him before he could recover and knocked him further back. The minute we made contact, the punches began.

Fist for fist, blow for blow. I was surprised he could take a guy like me.

The asshole also had an ace up his sleeve.

He pulled a pocket knife from the pocket in his sleeve and dug it into the bullet wound on my shoulder. It was so painful I cried out from it and saw stars again.

That gave him the upper hand, and he managed to get on top of me and pin me down.

He pulled the knife out and held it to my face.

"I should cut your face off and eat it. I think I'd love to display it on the front of my car though. Like a flag. On your cheek I'd write *idiot*."

"Fuck you." I tried to headbutt him, but he sliced across my cheek.

"You have the diamonds, don't you?" he sang.

I did. I had them in my jacket pocket. They'd stayed there, safe.

He went to move away my jacket, but I caught his hand and crushed it. That made him madder. He stuck the knife in again. Right into my wound. The damn wound was throwing me off my game. I should have been able to take him down easily, but then I realized why I was thrown. My arm felt numb, and suddenly, I couldn't feel the pain anymore. Or my arm.

Fucking bastard.

"Ahhhh, it's working. That arm of yours won't be any good to you for at least half an hour.

"What did you give me."

"Do you like it? I'm going to give you some more. I give it to all my meals that I keep alive as I eat them. Amelia's gonna get the same. Though she'll be dead by the time I get to eat her. I still want to save her tits. I was thinking I'd get a glass case made for them."

I growled at him and moved my good arm,

punching him hard. He punched back, and damn it, we both went tumbling down the next rung of steps. Without my arm it made it difficult to control myself.

I hit my head hard on the edge of the last step. That actually made me feel sick.

Again, Victor seized the opportunity and came at me. He pinned me using his legs around my arms. It was a lock I couldn't break out of.

But I had to.

I had to save Amelia. I had to save my girl.

Once again and for the second time today, I thought of how much I loved her. Both times were just before I thought death had come for me.

Victor pulled a gun from his back pocket and pulled the trigger.

"Time for you to go, boss," Victor taunted. "Time to—"

A gunshot sounded. I gasped when I saw the damn thing go through Victor's chest and wiz past my head.

Victor sucked in a breath and grabbed his chest.

"Blood. I actually have blood, and it's red. My mother told me that devil children had blood like tar. She lied, like with everything else." Another shot ripped into his chest, and blood splashed all over my face. When Victor skittered back, howling in pain, I saw Claudius coming down the stairs, gun in hand.

"The first one was for Henry, the second for Lydia." Claudius bellowed and shot him two more times. "That was for Jack and Susanna."

I was surprised Victor was still alive.

"Revenge." Victor gurgled blood and slumped against the railing on the stairs.

Claudius shot him again in the stomach. "That is for taking Amelia and Gigi and for all the shit you've dealt over the last few weeks."

Victor opened his mouth, but no words came out.

To my surprise, Claudius reached behind him and pulled out Victor's sword he'd dropped upstairs.

Victor's eyes went wide when Claudius raised it.

"This is for my brother. Fuck you for screwing with him!" Claudius swung the sword in a wide arc, hacking off Victor's head.

All I could do was stare.

All I could do was look at the dismembered body of Victor and his head as it dropped down the stairs. Grotesque.

Claudius looked at me. "No more blood on

your hands, brother, and not for him. Clean start for you. Justice is served. Now let's go find Amelia."

He reached out his hand to help me get up.

I looked back to Victor's body, closing that chapter of him in my mind and my life.

On to the next mission.

CHAPTER 18

Amelia

A gentle breeze caressed my cheeks.

I looked ahead, through the doors to the sunroom, and saw her.

Mom.

My heart danced with the elation of seeing her. She walked around the garden in that beautiful red dress that made her look like a beautiful blast from the forties.

The suave curl of her hair and her cherry red lips carried off the look.

"Mom," I called out to her, but she didn't hear me.

I called out again, getting closer, and she stopped smelling the long-stemmed English roses and turned to face me.

She really did look just like me. Or rather, I looked like her, except I had Dad's brown eyes.

She had bright blue eyes, almost like Luc, but his were almost turquoise.

She hugged me hard and stepped back to look me over.

"My dear girl, where have you been? Dinner's going to be cold, and you know how Millicent gets when anyone's late to dinner." She chuckled.

Dinner...

Millicent...

Mom...

Where was I? *When* was I?

This was a dream. Had to be.

The realization of that tugged on my emotions.

"I know." I didn't care. Dream or not, she was here. She was here, and she looked real to me. She felt real to me. So, it was her. For me, it was her.

"I feel like I haven't seen you in years." She cupped my face and smiled.

"You haven't. But it's okay."

"Come sit." She put her arm around me and

ushered me to the little bench beside the gazebo. "Tell me how your day was. And about the guy."

"My day just got better for seeing you. And... the guy is nice. Really nice. I love him. He's good to me."

"Good, that's all I want. Your father was good to me. But..." Sadness washed over her face. "I hurt him, Amelia. Don't make the same foolish mistakes I made and hurt the people who care about you. There is no excuse for that. It's all my fault. Everything that happened is all my fault."

"No, it's—" She didn't let me finish.

She shook her head at me and planted a kiss on my forehead. "It's my fault, sweet girl. Let's face it. It is, and you know that I know that. That's why we're here."

I opened my mouth to respond but stopped. I heard my name being called from far away. Far, far away.

Someone was calling me. My heart responded first, warming as it recognized the voice before my brain did.

Luc...

I looked around but couldn't see him.

"You need to wake up," Mom said. "Wake up and remember always that I love you."

"I love you," I told her, speaking from my heart.

She smiled, and darkness filled my surroundings.

"Amelia!" Luc cried out in a frantic voice. So hurried and panic stricken it snapped me out of the dream.

"Luc." My voice was barely audible, and my throat was dry. Dry like I'd just swallowed a handful of dirt. I tried to swallow, but I couldn't even do that.

I blinked several times trying to see my surroundings. The gentle breeze caressed my cheek, stinging my skin.

I was looking at a garden ahead of me. A vast expanse of wild flowers that hadn't been tended to in forever.

"Amelia!" Luc's voice again.

Now, I looked up and saw him. He was on the roof just ahead of me, standing about fifteen feet away. Claudius was with him.

Before them lay a vast expanse of rigid glass. On the roof. Not the kind you could walk across.

Wait... how did I miss that?

Where am I?

I made the mistake of looking down now and nearly fainted.

I screamed.

I was hanging from the roof of wherever I was, and below me was a drop of what I would say a hundred feet. A hundred feet right into the jagged rock formations that ran into the river.

I looked up to see two ropes were attached to me, wrapped around my arms and waist. They were attached to the bolts on the fixture on the roof. The ropes twined into one, and right there in the middle of the connection was a bomb.

An actual bomb.

"Fantastic," Tag's voice boomed just above me. He crouched down and smiled at me. "She's awake. Had to knock you out to pull off this little stunt of mine. Glad to see your boys are here."

"Let her go!" Luc cried. He tried to come across the glass, but Claudius held him back.

"The glass, Luc, wait," Claudius cautioned.

Looking properly now, I could see the glass had missing sections. It was a little different to where I was, although where I was didn't exactly look stable. I thought that part was intentional.

"Yes, Luc, the glass. I'm going to have to ask you to leave the diamonds over there and leave." Tag declared.

"Fuck you, asshole. You seriously think I'm just going to hand them over to you? Release Amelia."

Luc stood firm, vicious in his manner and expression.

He and Claudius both had that dark, vengeful look.

I couldn't believe they'd come for me.

"I'm sorry. This was never negotiable. You must have misunderstood. I wanted Amelia dead and to have possession of the diamonds. Not the diamonds in exchange for her life." Tag laughed.

"You give her to me, or you get nothing," Luc barked.

"Thought this might happen. Anyway, the answer's the same." Tag straightened and held out a remote control. "See this baby? It's the detonator for the bomb above your love's head. You will give the diamonds to me."

"Do you seriously have no form of dignity? You're an old fool."

"You're just like your father, Luc, *awkward*. An awkward brownnose who was little more than Raphael's lapdog."

"Why don't you come over here and say that closer to our faces," Claudius challenged.

"How about I let these guys answer that question for you?" Tag whistled, and from the platform just across from Luc, a host of guys emerged, coming up from downstairs. They all had guns.

Tears rolled down my cheeks.

God, this was it. Luc and Claudius would never make it.

I thought they would cower or something, but they didn't.

"Blood for blood!" Luc yelled.

What I saw next made me think I was still dreaming.

Max and Sinclaire came out first, firing shots that took out the first row of guys.

Max, my partner Max.

I never thought I'd see him again. *And Sinclaire.*

They were both here.

Behind them were The Four and Maurice. They managed to take down more guys. They might have been outnumbered, but they had enough skill to deal with Tag's men.

Luc and Claudius didn't join in. They were looking for a way across the roof. I watched them. While Luc looked, Claudius covered his back, shooting at anyone who got close.

"Bastards. I'll show them," Tag growled. He moved around the arc above us, so I could see him fully. "This will not end well for you. I want you dead more than I want those diamonds. I want you dead." He held the detonator out, so I could see it. "I think five minutes will give me enough time to dash."

As soon as the words left his mouth, a bullet ripped through his arm. I gasped.

It took him by complete surprise, and he dropped the detonator. I watched it drop all the way down and disappear amongst the rocks just below me.

Another bullet hit him, and we both turned to see where they were coming from.

Dad walked across the glass roof on our side. He'd come from a different direction than Luc.

"Fucking asshole, who do you think you are!" Dad bellowed.

Tag growled, propelling himself toward Dad, but he had to dodge when Dad fired more shots.

I looked at the two in complete horror. Dad looked like the person he'd been that night when he shot Agent Peterson. That was what he looked like. However, instead of the shock I'd felt that night, I felt triumph.

He'd come for me too.

"How dare you think you can hurt my daughter. You're dead! Son of a bitch." Dad screamed.

Tag took out his own gun and shot at him. Dad dodged it and jumped straight into Tag, knocking him over. I didn't know where he got the strength and the energy from. Days ago, he'd looked so frail.

The two started fighting, and bullets started firing as they tried to shoot each other. One went into the glass and broke it, causing that whole section of panels to give. As the fixture dangled, I realized how unstable it was. Rust had taken the areas around it.

Another bullet fired and went through the glass nearby.

"Amelia," Luc called to me.

I returned my gaze to him. He'd found a path and was inching across the roof.

"Luc, it's not safe. Go back. The glass... it's not safe." I would just die if the roof caved in and he fell through.

"Don't worry about me, goddess. I'll come for you."

I couldn't steady my breathing. It was too much. Too much going on around me. Too much.

Dad and Tag throwing punches at each other. Luc climbing across a glass roof with missing panels and a rusty framework.

Another set of glass panels gave way just beside me, and shit, it took out the bolt on the left holding me up.

I screamed as I dropped lower. Now, I couldn't see Luc at all, but I could see Dad.

"You took everything from me!" Tag yelled.

"Fucking prick. This is on you, not me." Dad barked back. They both had one gun now that they were fighting to gain control of.

Both had their hands on the handle. They maneuvered it down, and it went between them. Tag was on top of Dad, gaining control over him.

Across from me, everyone was still fighting. Bullets were being fired, everyone was shouting, but I heard that one single shot go off between Dad and Tag.

I screamed again when the two of them went still.

That moment seemed like forever. I watched it in complete horror, chills running down my spine in cold icy tendrils. Time froze right in front of me, like I'd pressed pause on the TV remote.

When Tag moved, my heart squeezed, but then he fluttered back, going limp.

It was him who got hit. Not Dad.

Not Dad.

Dad didn't even spare him another moment. He came for me. With his face battered and bruised, blood running from his nose, he came to me.

"There, there. It's going to be alright." He tried to smile.

"Dad." I winced.

"I know, I know. We can talk about this tomorrow. Let's just get home and out of this crazy mess."

I looked at him wondering how he was going to get to me.

Luc appeared in my view.

"Boss," Luc cried.

"Lucian, you have to go back. The glass is going to give."

"I'm going to jump across to you," Luc said.

I looked from Luc to Dad, seeing their love for me, and felt so complete in that moment.

But damn it, just like with everything since this whole crazy mess had started, there was never a dull moment. Never time to take a breath.

The bolt on the other fixture started to wobble, causing me to drop. Dad saw and leaned in to try and catch the rope, but he was too far up.

"Keep very, very still, Amelia. Please. No sudden moves."

"Okay... okay," I answered breathlessly.

"Raphael, let me come help. Move out the way!" Luc yelled.

"Luc, I'm warning you. Stay back. We don't

know what kind of impact you'll make jumping over here like that. We could all die. The panels aren't stable." Dad shook his head.

He leaned in again, this time suspending himself a little over the ledge, and swung in to catch the rope. He started pulling on the part that was just under the bolt. Pulling up with all his strength. I was lifted higher.

Dad pulled and pulled trying to get me up. I could see his struggle as he did so. Then the dreaded bolt came free completely, causing Dad to slip as I bobbled again.

I was surprised to see he regained his footing and continued pulling again. There was another bolt I didn't see just behind me. He managed to secure the rope onto that. He stopped for a second and grabbed his chest, breathing hard. It was too much for him.

"Dad, stop. Get to safety. Please. You can't do this." He couldn't. He had that frail look again.

"No. No. You let me take care of you," he cried. "I'm going to pull you up."

He pulled again, and I was almost up. It would have been so much easier if I hadn't been tied up the way I was with the ropes wrapped around my arms. He literally had to do all the work.

One last pull, and I would be right up there on

the roof with him, but the panels holding us up came free, and we both fell through the air as it crumbled.

"Daaaaadddd!" I screamed.

Dad rolled past me, and both Luc and I cried out.

I thought he was going to fall straight to the ground, but Dad grabbed the rope dangling below my legs.

Resilience and determination shone from his face. My breath hitched somewhere between my heart and my throat as I watched him climb up higher.

He didn't say anything; he just held on tight, pulled in a deep breath, then reached into his back pocket to pull out a knife.

"Dad, what are you doing?" I couldn't keep the panic out of my voice.

"Amore mio, listen to me. I'm cutting the rope from your arms. When it loosens, grab the rope above you and pull yourself up."

"No, I'll help you." I wiggled my fingers.

"Amelia, listen to me. Do this for me. Just focus."

"I can't. I won't leave you. Cut the rope from me, and I'll help you up first. Then you can pull me up."

"You get your stubborn from me, girl. Now's not the time to be stubborn. I need you to listen to me. Remember that day, that first day I took you to your first ballet class?"

I'd been five, but it was a day I would never forget. It was one of the most meaningful days of my life. "I remember." I whimpered.

"All the other girls were so good, and it threw you off. But I told you to do your own thing. Focus and do what comes to you. Focus. When you did, you did what came natural to you."

I started sobbing. The mask of the tough cop I'd become over the years faded, and I could have been that little girl again.

"Amelia, we need to act fast. Ready?"

I nodded, unable to talk.

He slid a little higher and started cutting away at the knots. My left arm came free first, and I reached up to grab the rope above me.

"I'm going to leave the rope around your waist, just in case."

My right arm came free, and I shook the remains of the rope from me. It fell down past Dad.

"Dad, I can pull the both of us up now." I was determined to.

The rope above us started to shift, then it

dropped slightly. The panel just before the bolt gave way, and we both dropped some more. I looked down at Dad, my heart beating so fast I thought it was going to jump out of my chest.

We were going to die. This wouldn't work.

"Lucian," Dad cried, glancing over his shoulder and locking his gaze with Luc's.

"Boss, no..."

The two seemed to share some hidden message I wasn't privy to.

"You and your brother are like sons to me. Your father is... he is like family. Tell him I said that."

"Tell him yourself. Raphael, son of a bitch. Don't you dare..." Luc wailed.

"I always liked that you called me Raphael. My mom used to hate when people shortened my name. You showed me respect always, and I appreciated it. Please take care of my little girl. She really loves you."

"No. Boss, no. Don't." Luc cried.

"Dad, what are you doing?" I cried, catching his attention.

He looked back to me and smiled. "Amore mio, the rope can't take the weight of the two of us. It can't, not for the two of us. Listen to me sweet girl and climb up."

As if on cue, we heard a crack. Dad held up his knife and smiled. A tear ran down his cheek.

"Dad, no!" I screamed. I knew just by looking at him what he meant to do. I knew it, but I didn't want to accept it.

"Amelia Rossi, remember when I said I'd love you with my last breath? I meant it."

With one slash, he cut through the rope above him and below my feet.

"Dad, noooo! Please take my hand. Papa!! Papa!"

Everything stilled around me, like time froze again. I watched horrified at what was happening.

Another slash severed the rope. It severed the rope with a snap, and Dad was falling away from me.

He looked up at me as he went down.

Falling away...

Falling... away.

Falling...

It happened so fast. It all happened so fast.

One minute he was there, and the next he was falling away from me.

My father...

He'd cut himself free from the rope to save me.

My screams echoed all around. Inside and outside of me.

CHAPTER 19

Amelia

"Amelia!" Luc cried.

I couldn't look at him. I couldn't look away from where Dad had fallen.

Although I couldn't see where he landed, I didn't want to look away. It felt like letting go. Letting go of him.

I couldn't let go.

"Amelia, you have to climb up, please. Don't let your dad's sacrifice be in vain. Please," Luc pleaded.

I couldn't answer through my sobs.

"He did so much for you." He reminded. "So much to protect you, so much to make it possible for you to live the life you wanted. Please, climb up."

His words gripped me to my core. Dad had done so much for me. Right from the very beginning when I'd found out about our family and the secret life we'd lived.

He'd made sure I had what I wanted, protected me and loved me with his last breath.

That crack sounded again and fueled me with strength.

Dad had loved me with his last breath and given me another chance to live.

I couldn't let his last sacrifice be in vain. I pulled in a sharp breath to clear my head and grabbed on tightly to the rope. Then, with one hand after the other, I used all my upper body strength to climb up.

Up I went until I was above the panel by the bolt the rope was attached to.

"That's it. Now, get off the roof," Luc called out.

"Luc. My dad…"

"I know, darling… I know." I looked beyond him. The fighting had stopped, and our men were all standing looking on in sadness. Even Sinclaire and Max. "Go on now, Amelia. I'll come get you." He nodded.

A fresh bout of tears took me, but I gathered my strength and moved across the panels. I wasn't out of the woods yet. I moved past Tag, not bothering to spare a moment to look at him. I didn't want to. I didn't need to.

I could see it. The steps leading down from the roof. The whole thing started to shake, and the panels around all cracked and fell in. I had to jump to make it over the side with the steps.

Instantly, I looked back to Luc, who'd watched me until I was safe.

It was only then that he started to move back. I watched him too, making sure he was safe, holding my breath until he got to his side.

He raised his hand and waved to me.

It was over.

My gaze fell to the drop again, and tears took me, uncontrollable and overpowering.

Dad.

I couldn't believe what had happened.

It didn't feel real. It didn't feel right.

He was gone.

It took Luc and Claudius fifteen minutes to get to me. I never stopped crying.

I seemed to pass out from it, and when I woke up, a bright light blinded me.

I squinted against it, blinked, then refocused. Blinked again.

Luc stood beside my bed… no … I got them mixed up again.

Sometimes Luc and Claudius looked so much alike. It wasn't until I saw his eyes—one blue and the other brown, and then the cross on his cheek—that I realized it wasn't Luc.

Next to Claudius was Marcus. Then Gigi, Max, and Sinclaire.

I looked around me. I was in the hospital. I tried to sit up, but something was attached to my arm. Wires that went to a drip bag and monitors.

"Easy there, pet. You need your rest," Marcus said, offering a kind smile.

"Why am I here? I'm fine."

"No, you aren't. You have a broken rib, and you were severely dehydrated," Claudius answered. "The doctors wanted to keep you for observation."

I looked at everyone. "Thank you all so much for coming."

"Don't mention it," Max replied.

"Like we wouldn't," Sinclaire offered. "Next time, if the damn golden eagle isn't riding the horse, promise me you won't tell me it is."

"I promise." I gave him a weak smile and looked to Gigi, who moved closer to take my hand.

She looked a little off. In fact, they all did, and I looked around them for Luc.

He wasn't there. "Where's Luc?"

When Gigi's eyes filled with a wealth of sadness, I knew something else had happened. Something more.

"Amelia." Marcus cleared his throat. "Victor leaked some stuff to the feds, and the police came to take Luc away this morning."

My eyes widened, and I sucked in a sharp breath. "What? No, what stuff?"

"How about you rest up, and we talk about it in a little while. Doctors said you may be good to come home tomorrow."

"No, I want to talk now." My heart started galloping, and my muscles tensed.

"Trust me, princess," Claudius intoned. "It's best not to."

I looked from him to Sinclaire and Max. Both had that solemn look on their faces.

It told me everything.

Luc was a mobster. Of course, he should be locked up.

What did I expect?

~

Luc

~

I was surprised I hadn't ended up here before now.

Very surprised.

I guess it was just a matter of time before I got what was coming to me.

Me behind bars.

I was sitting on the metal bench of a jail cell at the Chicago Police Department. I wasn't where I should have been. With Amelia, by her side, making sure she was okay. Or even with my men, grieving our losses. We came out strong but we took hits and several guys lost their lives.

I was here now.

Helpless. Again.

The guy opposite me was just staring at the wall.

When I came in yesterday, he'd looked at me

like he recognized me but said nothing. Not a damn thing.

I didn't care.

What I cared about now was the uncertainty of this situation I'd found myself in.

My dear friend Victor had dealt his last blow. The last thing he could do to screw with me.

He'd gotten to one of our contacts in the feds and threatened his family if he didn't leak info on some of the rackets I'd run over the past year.

The guy had leaked, and about an hour after we'd arrived at the hospital with Amelia, I got taken away. Handcuffed and led away out in the open like the criminal I was.

They'd been looking for me.

The ironic thing was, I'd taken off my jacket and given it to Claudius just before the doctors took me away to examine my arm. The jacket had the diamonds in the inside pocket.

Dad and Claudius had tried to intervene when the cops came, trying to talk them away, but it was useless. They couldn't do anything. No one could.

Now, I was here awaiting something I didn't know what, and no one—friend nor family—was allowed to see me.

I looked up as the guard approached the cell door. Behind him was Sinclaire.

God, why?

He was the last person I wanted to see right now.

This had to be the classic case of kicking a man while he was already down.

"You got fifteen minutes," the guard told Sinclaire.

He came in and sat on the chair opposite me.

"What are you doing here?" The void inside me didn't have the strength to be an asshole to him.

"How you holding up?" He asked to my surprise.

"Doesn't matter." Physically, I was functional. They'd tended to the wound on my arm back at the hospital. Mentally… I couldn't really speak for my mental state right now. "Why are you here, Sinclaire? You're the last person I expected to come see me. You here to gloat? To tell me how you're better than me? That Amelia can do better with you than me? You know what? Save it. You're right. She can, and she should be with you."

He started laughing and straightened. "Amelia loves you, Luc. I'm jealous of you for that, but she's my friend, and more than that. She's like family, close to me like that, and I'm not here to gloat or tell you shit you don't need to hear."

"I'm behind bars. You know what the sentencing for racketeering is? A max of twenty years. *Twenty years.*" I shook my head.

"I'll see what I can do. Whatever it is. I came to find out one thing first. Make sure you answer this wisely."

"What is it?"

"Back at the prison, I watched you crawl on the roof, and damn, those panels weren't safe at all. Most were missing. But you did it without thinking of yourself. It was then that I realized you must really love her. You looked like you would do anything for her. I came here to hear it for myself. Do you love her?"

I had to sit up straighter. I couldn't believe his question, but I'd give him my answer.

"I love her more than life itself. I love her enough to do anything for her, and enough to ask you to take care of her and to make sure she's happy. Make sure she gets her dream back and doesn't slip away in the shadows."

He nodded. "Okay."

"That all?" I narrowed my gaze at him.

"Yeah." He stood up and signaled for the guard to open the door.

He left, and I returned to my former hollowness.

Back to the void.

~

Two more days passed before I got to see Amelia.

She sat amongst the visitors in the public gallery. Next to her were Claudius, Pa, and Sinclaire.

I sat with my lawyer at the defense table. Across from us was a badass prosecuting lawyer called Simms. I'd had a run-in with him a couple of times.

Presiding was Judge Montpellier. I'd never seen him before or heard of him.

He looked at me like he didn't like the look of me.

I stared at Amelia, wishing I could hold her one last time. Wishing and praying, but I knew that was just a dream.

A woman like that was always a dream to me.

Raphael had asked me to take care of his daughter, but look at me. Right now, I couldn't even take care of myself.

The judge cleared his throat, and I returned my focus to him.

"Okay, this is going to be quick unless there is any further evidence that needs to be considered."

He looked from Simms to my lawyer. Both shook their heads. "Will the defendant please rise." He focused his eyes on me.

I felt nervous and helpless as I stood. Damn, was I ever the shadow of the man I used to be. The big bad from Chicago. Lucian Morientz.

Fuck.

Judge Montpellier cleared his throat. "I've deliberated over the charges presented, and this is my ruling. The evidence is substantial and irrefutable. So, Lucian Morientz, you are guilty as charged in line with the Racketeer Influenced and Corrupt Organizations Act. The defendant acted knowingly and intentionally in contravention to the laws set out by this Act. As such, the Court is prepared to proceed to sentencing. Since the defendant has no prior convictions of this nature, I see this as a level nineteen offence. So, I sentence you to thirty-seven months in prison."

Well, at least it wasn't twenty years.

If they'd gotten all the dirt on the old me, it might have been life.

I said the old me because the guy who did all that shit wasn't me anymore.

I looked back at Amelia, who was crying. Claudius had his arm around her.

"I'm sorry," I said although she couldn't hear me.

She read my lips though and shook her head. "I love you," she mouthed back.

Three years and one month.

I was sure I'd die. It had been hard to be without her for just the few days I hadn't seen her.

This would be the straw that broke my back.

CHAPTER 20

Amelia

It started to rain. Just like last time. Ironic.

Another funeral.

Another parent.

Mom... now Dad.

Last time, the rain fell, and I stood by Mom's grave until I was drenched. I couldn't leave. I did the same thing now, unable to leave with the other guests who were departing from the cemetery.

My eyes were fixed on the grave. The dirt had been laid, and Dad buried. He had a beautiful ceremony with close to a thousand people in attendance. It was like a state funeral.

The closest went to watch the burial. That included all his men who were left after the battle, and me.

There were so many people around me, but I felt all alone. So very alone.

It was worse than when Mom died.

This was worse.

It was worse because they were both gone. Because it felt like I'd just found Dad only to lose him. I'd just started to understand him, just started to forgive him. As I'd hung from that rope, I'd willed myself to make it, so I could take care of him for the rest of his life, however long he had left. I saw me doing that and having more time to make up for lost time. I didn't realize that I would have to say goodbye then.

I'd said goodbye forever to him and Millicent, both in the same day.

Millicent's funeral was on Sunday.

I'd also had to practically say goodbye to Luc no less than twenty-four hours later.

I couldn't believe that after all we'd been through, this was the result.

A whole week had passed since Luc's sentencing. He'd been transferred to the Metropolitan

Correctional Center, and we still weren't allowed to see him.

We had visitation planned for two days' time, but it felt like forever.

Two days, then once a month.

Once a month for the next three years and one month.

God...

This was hard.

It was all hard.

Someone put an arm around me. I looked up at Marcus and nodded. I'd cried so much over the last few days that I had nothing left in me. I was an empty well of nothingness.

"Come on, pet. It's time to go." He glanced up at the rain as it came down heavier.

"I can't leave. Not yet. I don't want to say goodbye."

"Pa, I'll stay with her," Claudius offered.

Gigi came up to us, followed by Max and Sinclaire.

"I can stay too," she said, reaching out to take my hand.

"Us too," Max offered, and Sinclaire nodded.

"Well, I guess I'm staying too," Marcus intoned, pressing his thin lips together. He held his umbrella over my head. "Raphael would have my head if I allowed his girl to catch a cold."

That did it. Hearing that made me cry the tears I didn't think I had left.

I practically collapsed into his arms, crying all that was left of me, for everything.

"You sure you're going to be okay in this big old house?" Sinclaire asked.

We sat in the living room of Dad's house... my house.

My house.

My home.

I guess it was mine.

It was home. It felt like home.

"I will. I'll be okay, maybe." I didn't know when that would be, but I was aiming for positivity.

Max shuffled next to Sinclaire and looked at me. "Kid, you know you can tell us if you're not okay. Plus, we can tell. I'm good to stay another week or longer."

"Me too," Sinclaire offered.

They were leaving today. They'd probably already stayed long enough.

"No." I shook my head at both of them.

"Well, I personally don't know how I'm supposed to get back to life without you in LA." Sinclaire chuckled.

"There is no life without me. Brad Sinclaire, you better call me every chance you get, and visit. I'll visit too. Don't you dare forget me." While I hadn't officially said it, they knew I wasn't going back to LA. They knew I was going to stay here.

Pick up where I left off, so to speak.

"You bet, Amelia. *Taylor.* You know, I never thought that name suited you. I like Rossi."

"Me too," Max agreed.

"I can't believe you guys came for me."

"We will always be there for you. Always," he promised. "I'm real sorry about everything. Including Jefferson and Holloway."

Neither of us had mentioned them. It was too painful.

I shook my head again. "It's fine. We have each other."

"We do. We also have something to tell you." Max smiled.

"What?"

"We did something really bad, so, whatever we're saying now has to stay in this room." Sinclaire looked around pretending to look shifty. "Who's here?" He lowered his voice.

"Gigi's upstairs casting runes." She was. My best friend was upstairs casting runes and spells. She'd annoyed Claudius so much earlier he had to leave the house.

"Okay, good, she needs to stay upstairs. This is top secret shit." Sinclaire nodded.

"Yes, we went rogue," Max agreed.

I actually laughed. I couldn't believe it. "What did you guys do?"

"Become mobsters."

"Jesus Christ. Now's not the time to joke around."

"I'm not joking. Listen, we might have been able to get a reduction of Luc's sentence."

My mouth dropped, and I sucked in a sharp breath. "What? How? Really?"

Sinclaire held up his hands. "Don't get your hopes up too high. We don't know if it panned out yet. But let's just say Judge Montpelier has been a really bad boy and we found out some stuff."

"Yeah, some pretty bad stuff." Max smirked.

"What? What stuff? You have to tell me."

"I'm afraid that's as much as we can say. We found out some stuff and handed it to Claudius, and Roose will be issuing a statement on behalf of our police department, showing how Luc helped capture Demarco and dismantled that whole drug ring. It will help. There's also the fact that he took down Victor, who is actually on the nation's most wanted list. It's all in his good books."

"Oh my gosh." My hands flew up to my cheeks. "You guys, I can't believe you did all that for me."

"Like we said, we'll always be there for you." Max stood, signaling that it was time to go. "I'm going to get our bags in the car. Gives you two a chance to talk without me."

He looked from me to Sinclaire and smiled. I stood up and gave him a hug.

"I'll call you when we land."

"You better." He left, and Sinclaire stood up. He brought his hands together and looked slightly nervous.

"I'll miss you. I'll miss you a lot." He nodded.

"I'll miss you too, Sinclaire." I gazed openly at him, at the man whom I probably should have been with but wasn't. There were so many good things about him, but I figured it out. More than the fact that I was in love with Luc and not him. I think it was because we were more than that.

"It was hard when I first went to LA. Hard lying to everyone I met. Hard lying to you. I was someone else. I always thought I was closer to Max than you, but I was wrong. It was you. I hated lying. I'm sorry, and I'm sorry it didn't work for us."

I felt I should explain that because it really affected him.

"Don't be. Don't be sorry. I acted like a real ass for a long time, but I was jealous. I came to the conclusion that I'd rather have you in my life as a friend than not have you at all."

"I'd rather have you as a friend too, but please don't think I never valued you, or didn't care."

"I never thought that, Amelia. Not once." He brushed his finger lightly across my jaw. "So, what now? You aren't a cop."

"I'm not a cop." I'd handed in my resignation a few days ago.

"You should have been a dancer. I always thought you moved like one."

"People said I walked like a cop."

"No, I saw beneath it all. I saw that there was more to you than what met the eye, but hey, I still get to find out. I'll come back in a few weeks."

"Really?" That surprised me.

"Yeah. I thought we could go see a basketball game or something. That's me being a friend." His smile brightened.

"I know."

"Come here."

I threw my arms around him and gave him a hug, one that lingered.

Max came back in, and Sinclaire released me.

He planted a light kiss on my forehead and moved to join him.

"Catch you later, boss lady."

I blew a kiss at them both.

I sat back down in the sofa and put my feet up. I just started to get comfortable when Gigi came in.

"Are the guys gone?" she asked.

"Yeah. It's just you and me, and I guess I'll be here by my lonesome in this house when you leave next week."

She shook her head. "No. Amelia, I didn't want to tell you this, but days ago, when I cast my cards, I was told that great fortune awaited me in a distant land, and I would be needed to help a friend in need."

"Okay, what does that mean? Clearly, I must be the friend in need, right? So, you can tick that box."

"Well, this felt like something new on the horizon for both of us. Anyway, we can work out how helpful I'll be as the days go by. Until we know, I wanted to tell you that I'm not going back to LA."

I straightened instantly. "What do you mean?"

"Well, we've always lived together. Not that I'm

saying we should live together forever, but I was thinking we could live here together. It would be cool, if you want to." She gave me a tentative smile.

Excitement and hope bubbled within me at the prospect of her staying. Of course I set out to do this all on my own but having her here would be the best ever. I thought maybe it would make it easier somehow. "Of course I want you to stay. I would love for you to, but what about the gallery and art? Your coven is in LA."

"They'll be fine with me leaving. We're supposed to do good. Plus, I think I'm needed here. I checked out a few art galleries, and two have gotten back to me. It looks hopeful. So, I figured I could stay here. You know, until Luc gets back."

"Three years and one month?" My voice shook as I spoke. I prayed whatever Sinclaire and Max had done helped in some way. I knew Luc was guilty, and it was wrong for me to wish he wasn't in prison, but that didn't stop me. So, I was going to be selfish and hope his sentence could be decreased.

"Three years and one month. We can see what happens."

"Gigi, that would be amazing. Thank you so much. I really need you."

"You are very welcome. Now, to find out what great fortune awaits. Chicago is the distant land."

"You know we're kind of rich, right?"

"We?"

I nodded. "What's mine's yours." Dad had left me all his possessions in Chicago and Italy. I didn't want to even contemplate what all that meant and what it was worth. I knew it was billions. Billions aside from the business. The business he'd given to Luc, who'd given it to Claudius. That existed outside what I had, and outside of me. I didn't have to do anything where it was concerned, and I didn't have to think about it. "Plus, I'm still trying to make amends for what happened to you."

"No, that isn't something you have to make amends for. Not one bit. Anyway, I'm over that and thrilled you want to share your wealth with me. I'm here to support you. It's been a difficult time for you, and I will be here as long as you need me."

"Thank you from the very bottom of my heart."

"Again, you are very welcome. How are you feeling?"

"Awful. It's too much."

"It will get better with time, and remember, every day that goes by is one day less that you'll have to wait for Luc."

That sounded hopeful. As with Max and Sinclaire, I didn't have to tell her that I would be staying here, but more importantly, I'd be waiting for Luc.

"That gives me something to look forward to."

"It does. Let me get dinner started before Claudius comes back. He brought a dead squirrel in the house the other night. So gross." She wrinkled her nose and frowned. "At least he'll have something to eat when he comes back."

I rolled my eyes and chuckled slightly. Claudius was quite a character. He had the whole tough guy image down to the T, but he'd barely left my side since I'd come home from the hospital. It was nice.

"I think he kind of likes the squirrels, but don't tell him I said that."

"What do you want to eat?"

"Bread."

"Bread with something else Amelia. You can't live on bread."

"I can't eat anything. I'm still sick from the crap they gave us back in the prison." I hadn't been able to hold anything down and had lost weight in just a handful of days.

"I'll make you chicken soup." She got up.

My phone started ringing, buzzing on the

coffee table. I winced, still anxious to answer it. I didn't think anyone could blame me. I looked at the screen and saw it was the hospital again. They'd been calling and leaving messages to contact them. I'd been putting it off because of everything that was going on.

Dad's funeral, Luc's trial, Millicent's funeral in a few days' time. The last thing I wanted was to be drawn off to the hospital or something medical.

I guess though, now that everything was over, I could take care of myself.

Gigi nodded at me as I answered the phone, and she left me.

"Hello."

"Hi, is this Miss Rossi?" came a soft feminine voice.

"Yes, speaking." I adjusted the phone at my ear.

"Hi, I'm Doctor Ferguson at the Chicago General. You are a very difficult woman to get hold off." She chuckled.

"I'm sorry. I had a lot of things to sort out. It's been a stressful time." That was probably putting it mildly.

"Well, stress is one thing you don't need right now."

"No, I agree."

"Well, that's a good start. I'm contacting you today because it was revealed in the tests we conducted while you are with us that you are pregnant."

At first, I didn't quite hear what she said. Then it hit me. It hit me hard, like someone had thrown a truck at me.

"I'm sorry. Can you repeat that?" I narrowed my eyes and pressed the phone closer to my ear.

"Congratulations, Miss Rossi, you're pregnant."

CHAPTER 21

Luc

～

"You look like shit," Claudius said, looking me over with disdain.

It was typical of him to point out the obvious.

I knew I looked like shit with my black swollen eyes and bruises all over my face.

"What the hell happened to you?" Pa asked.

I sighed with frustration. "Six guys jumped me. Romanos boys. Pricks." I wouldn't last in here. Not because I couldn't take care of myself, but because I couldn't control myself. Those assholes thought they could pick a fight with me because it was them against me. They were wrong.

They'd come at me when I was eating the filth they called lunch in this shithole. I took them down effortlessly, but that had landed me in solitary confinement for two days.

"You okay? I mean, are you hurt?" Pa asked.

"I'm alive. You should see the other guys." They had broken arms and legs.

This place was killing my soul, undoing all the good I'd done in the last few months. It was undoing me, the man I'd become since meeting Amelia.

I needed her. This was the first day I was allowed visitors, and I was going to tell her straight that she needed to move on with her life. Not that I assumed she would wait for me. I was just hoping. Hoping with my stupid heart, but at the same time thinking with my brain for a change.

I needed to let her go.

I sat with Pa and Claudius around a table in the visitors' lounge. There were guards everywhere.

Amelia was somewhere in the building waiting to see me next.

I was only allowed two visitors at a time. I guess it was good, though, to get to see her by herself. This would be the first time I got to speak to her in what seemed like forever.

I was so desperate to see her. Desperate to see how she was. I couldn't believe I'd missed Raphael's funeral. She had support, but I hadn't been there. Everyone else had been there for her but me.

"Well, we can now update you on the diamonds." Claudius straightened. "I handed them over to the Smithsonian Institute personally yesterday."

I was proud to hear that. "Thank you." Once upon a time neither of us would have thought to hand them over. We would have kept them.

"We just wanted them gone." Pa huffed and frowned. "Caused a lot of trouble."

"Didn't they just." I agreed.

"Too much, we can forget them now and start rebuilding." Claudius added bringing his hands together.

I was happy to hear that too. "Rebuilding?" I looked from him to Pa.

"Well son, we can pretty much do whatever we wat from here onwards. For good or bad. Don't expect us to become cops though." Pa chuckled.

"Don't even mention that cop word to me."

Claudius sneered. "Anyway, diamonds aside we have some news."

"What kind of news?"

"Good and bad. Two good pieces of news, actually."

I didn't know what kind of news would be good for me here. "Let's hear it." I leaned forward onto the table.

"First piece of news is, Maria contacted us. She said she's safe in Florida and sends her thanks." Claudius quirked a brow. "*And* her love. Didn't know you two saw each other recently."

"She helped me when I was looking for Victor."

"That all she did?"

I frowned at him. "Fuck, Claudius, now's not the time. I didn't do anything with her. Those days are gone."

"Good, that leads me to good news number two. We managed to reduce your sentence."

All I could do was stare. "Jesus Christ, how?" Yes, how indeed. How in the world had they managed that?

Claudius leaned in closer and spoke in a low, even tone. "Your cop boys from LA got some dirt on the judge. They also threw in your good deeds from LA. Catching Demarco and all that stuff.

However, the bad news is this. The sentence has been reduced to eight months with ten months community service, but on the basis of good behavior. That's the best we could do to make it look legit. "

I ran my hand across my face. Sinclaire. He had done this. He and Max, most probably. This was what he'd been talking about. God. I'd never imagined him doing anything for me. That guy quite rightly hated my guts.

And... eight months with community service?

Eight months with community service. I would take that over three years.

Definitely, but...

It was still too long. It was still too long to have any expectation from Amelia. She shouldn't have to wait, and I shouldn't dare contemplate it. I was a criminal, and in true criminal style, I was in prison. Locked up and out of her world. She could do better than that. Even if her waiting for me really was a possibility, I didn't know if I could commit wholly to the good behavior part. It wouldn't be because I didn't want to. The people here were all assholes. Staff and prisoners alike.

With the way how things were with me already banished to solitary confinement, I didn't know what the next eight months would bring.

Amelia shouldn't have to deal with that.

"Lucian, this is good news," Pa pointed out seeing my hesitation.

"Sure, it's the best."

He and Claudius exchanged worried glances.

"What's the matter with you?" Claudius asked. "It still sucks. I know it still sucks, but it's better than three years. Three years and one month."

"She can't be with me." That was the bottom line. "Claudius, make sure she gets back to LA safely."

Claudius laughed and stood up. "Look, brother, I'll see you at next month's visit."

I frowned at his lackadaisical attitude. I was being serious. More than serious. I was facing reality and stepping out of the bubble of the dream I'd created when I was with Amelia.

"Claudius." I called to him but he ignored me.

I watched him walk away, then turned back to face Pa, who was already giving me a pensive look.

"You know, as much as I adore her and had my loyalty to Raphael, I was against this made-up union between the two of you. You and Amelia. Right from that day when Raphael called us into his office and gave you his stipulations to take over the business. I was against it because I didn't want my kid being dragged into some arranged marriage. I was against it, and I was against the fact that you wanted to give up everything for her. I don't have to explain why because you know what I went through with your mother. *You* know what you went through with your mother. But Lucian, this turned into something else. You have to admit that. It turned into something else. Falling in love is never part of a plan. It just happens. Don't lose it. Think. Think about what you're doing." He rose and stood, still staring at me, still giving me that look. That look that burned straight into my soul.

He left too, leaving me to my thoughts.

Amelia would be in next.

There was so much to say, and I didn't know how to say it. Or what to say.

Where did I begin?

The door opened again, and in she came. The guard by the door pointed to me.

As I looked at her, everyone else faded into the background, everything faded into the background, and it was like we were the only two people here.

I stood up as she moved to me. Her hair was down, hanging in long velvet waves about her shoulders, curling up at the edge of her elbows.

The peach summer dress she wore flirted with

her legs. It was so unlike the cop version of her. Back when I'd met her, she would have never worn anything like that with so much color. She looked beautiful. She didn't look like Amelia Taylor anymore.

This was Amelia Rossi as herself, without the shadow of the past that haunted her.

When she got closer, she quickened her pace and ran straight into my arms, and instinctively, we kissed. Kissed like we always did when we saw each other. This was a kiss, though, of longing and love. A kiss to soothe a wounded soul.

I was only reminded of where we were when the guard came over to scold us for the contact.

"Do not kiss the prisoner," the large meatheaded man barked. "Public displays of affection are not allowed."

The roughness in his voice made Amelia jump.

"I'm sorry," she quickly apologized.

That was what I meant. Hearing someone speak to her like that pissed me off, but I controlled myself.

"Doll." I smiled at her.

She reached up and touched my face. Caressing my jaw with the softness of her fingertips.

I could have stood here forever. Forever in this moment. I loved her, and since I loved her, I had to do what was right for her.

"Sit, please." I ushered her to sit on the bench in front of me, where Claudius and Pa had previously sat.

"You look awful." She winced. "What happened?"

"Guys jumped me. It's fine. Don't worry about me, goddess. How've you been?"

She nodded and smiled, but the smile never reached her eyes. "I'm trying."

"I'm sorry I couldn't be there for you. For your father's funeral."

"No, you can't be sorry for that." She shook her head, and I couldn't help but look at her long, elegant neck and the silky-smooth skin along the curve of her shoulders.

"If I weren't such a bad person, I would have been there for you, right?"

"You aren't a bad person."

"I'm guilty, Amelia."

"Luc, you must know about the reduction of the sentence." She nodded.

"I know. But it doesn't change anything." I bit the inside of my lip.

"It changes the time from three years to eight months. That's significantly different."

I stared at her. This was the part where I was supposed to tell her to move on. I was supposed to tell her that love wasn't enough and that she could and should do better than me.

How did you tell the woman of your dreams all of that?

How would I do it?

"You can't be with me." That was how. "Goddess, you... can't and shouldn't be with me."

She stared at me as if I'd just slapped her in her face. She held my gaze for what seemed like eons before she spoke.

"Why?" Her eyes continued to bore into my soul.

"You deserve better, and I would be lying if I told you I love you and not tell you the truth."

Her breathing stilled, and a tear ran down her cheek. "Then don't lie to me and tell me that's what you truly believe. Don't do it, Luc, don't. It's eight months. It's nothing."

"It's not just the waiting. It's everything. The waiting is the cherry on top, and damn, I can't promise good behavior when there are people here out to kill me if they can. I've seen this before. The littlest thing I do to defend myself, and that chance for a reduced sentence will be taken away from me."

She shook her head again. "Well, you will promise me good behavior. It's the least, and it's nothing. I chose you. I *choose* you. It means the good and the bad. It means everything. I don't want to be with anyone else. You're it for me, so don't you dare tell me you can't promise good behavior and tell me bullshit about me doing better. There is no better than what your heart wants. Don't you dare take another dream away from me."

"*Dream?*" I couldn't believe her words were for me, or the depth of her love for me.

"I dream, always of being with you Lucian. I need you." She pulled in a labored breath. "*We* need you," she added. Her voice was on the edge of a breath.

I tried to make light of the situation as I processed this. "They don't need me, goddess. They all take care of themselves. Jesus, look at Claudius. He's boss, what more can I say? And Pa never needed anyone ever anyway. Maurice is wrapped up in Gigi and –"

"No, not them." She interrupted and her cheeks flushed. "Us."

I didn't know what she meant until she slipped her hand over her stomach.

Then a sudden coldness hit my core, and a flush of adrenaline coursed through my body.

My heart raced. My mouth fell open.

I... moved to her, dropped to my knees, and pressed my hand to her stomach.

Her tear-filled eyes met mine.

"Amelia, what are you saying to me?" I gazed long and hard at her. I dared not allow the thought of what she was saying to enter my mind. Things like that were too good for me.

Family. My own...

"I'm... pregnant. My, um... pills, um, birth control ran out before I got to Chicago." She started to cry, and I hoped like hell she didn't think I was mad. "With everything going on, I forgot I needed them, and I... I'm sor—"

I placed a finger on her lips. "No, no. Don't say it. Don't tell me you're sorry. This is more than a dream for a guy like me."

"Really?"

"Oh yes, yes, yes." Although my hands were shaking, I took hold of hers.

"You can't let me deliver this baby by myself. I don't want to do this without you. We need you." She held my gaze.

"And I will be there. I will be there for you both, Amelia Rossi, because you are mine."

For the first time in my life, a strong sense of purpose filled my soul. It mixed with the love I felt for her.

I would be there for her and be the kind of man she deserved.

The kind of man *they* deserved.

Eight months later...

It had felt like this day would never come.

It felt like a forever ago since I'd made that promise to Amelia, and while I'd seen her every month when she visited, it almost felt like I hadn't seen her.

It was torture not being with her, torture watching her stomach grow and not being there to take care of her the way I wanted.

Torture just getting pictures of my baby's scans and not seeing him.

Him.

We were having a boy, and we decided it was fitting to call him Raphael. We both came up with the idea. It felt honorable. I liked that.

Raphael Lucian Morientz. That was to be his name.

At least I got to have a hand in naming him.

It felt like torture not being there after for both of them.

But...

Today was the day that all changed. Today was the day when I'd shed my old life, this place, and all that I used to be.

Today was the day when I was going to be the man my goddess deserved and the kind of father my boy could look up to.

As I took that walk down the corridor that led outside the correctional facility, hope filled my soul.

The hope that came with a second chance. A second chance I desperately wanted.

I was reminded of that game I'd played once with Amelia when we'd first met.

The game of leaving behind the world and becoming anything I wanted to be.

This was real. No games. It really was real, and I could be anything now.

I'd had to put up with all manner of shit while

inside just to secure this moment, because it was worth it. She was worth it.

They were worth it.

And there she was...

As I emerged from the door, the door I'd only seen once in eight months, I saw her.

She stood by her car waiting for me. Pregnancy was a good look on her, and she'd grown even bigger than the last time I saw her.

Beautiful, my goddess.

She moved to me at the same time I moved to her. I wanted to pick her up and hug her hard, but I settled for the contact I got from holding her and our precious baby between us.

"Luc, you did it." Tears ran down her cheeks.

I didn't care what I looked like, but I started crying too. "I did. I promise you this will never happen to us again. I swear it."

"I know. I know."

I cupped her face, then lowered to my knees to kiss her stomach. "Thank you for waiting for me."

"As if I wouldn't. I love you, Lucian Morientz."

I couldn't have felt more awe at her heartfelt words. "I love you too, and I am going to spend the rest of my life making you happy."

"Thank you. That works, because I plan to do the same thing to you."

"You don't have to do anything."

"Well, it's too late. I already went shopping and bought you a bonsai tree."

I laughed. "Really?"

"Hmmm mmmm. It needs butterflies though," she giggled.

"Okay, goddess, anything else we need?"

"Just each other."

That sounded like everything I could ever want.

EPILOGUE

Luc

Two years later

"You know, I don't know how you do it." Maurice eyed Sinclaire dangerously.

I'd caught him watching Sinclaire full of suspicion all afternoon. The same way he did whenever he saw him.

He was doing the same thing now as my boy, Raphael, chased Sinclaire around the rose bush. I chuckled at the spectacle. Raphael could barely run on his little legs, but Sinclaire pretended to look terrified.

Claudius, Maurice, and I had been sitting on the terrace for the last hour watching them.

Amelia was out teaching her weekend ballet class.

This was something we did regularly and definitely when Sinclaire came to visit. We'd have drinks and watch the baby try to catch him.

"How do I do what?" I asked, knowing what he meant but just messing with him.

"He means have the cop here who wanted your woman and probably wants to steal your son," Claudius filled in, sipping on his beer. He quirked a brow and narrowed his eyes at me.

"Do you know how ridiculous that sounds?" I challenged.

"Yes. Course I do. The man's still after your woman and he wants to steal your baby. Woman first though."

"Do you see Amelia here?"

"That doesn't mean squat," Maurice jumped in, curling his lips under in distaste. "She's teaching. He knows what time she'll be back. Also, I saw him at the school, hanging around outside like a creeper."

"What were you doing at the school? Signing up for dance lessons?" I laughed. "Pretty certain Amelia could give you a one-on-one and have you doing leaps through the air in no time. Come Christmas, you could be the sugar plum fairy."

Even Claudius laughed at that.

"Very funny, wise guy. I was actually following him." Maurice smirked.

"You don't need to do that. What would you have done if Amelia caught you?"

"Dance, and style it out." He nodded.

"Right." Claudius shook his head. "I can just imagine you doing that. She'd probably slap you for making a mockery of her profession."

Like always, talking about dancing made me think of how much Amelia loved it. My wife loved dancing, and I was so proud to tell anyone who asked that she was a teacher and ran her own dance school. Her own dance school here in Chicago and a summer school in Italy I'd built for her on the grounds of the vineyard, where I set up business to procure the finest wine and grow the most exotic bonsai trees.

That's what I did now for a living. Both there and Chicago. I put myself and my skills to good use, and true to his word, Maurice followed me wherever I went. He'd given up the mobster life too and worked with me.

"I still don't trust him," Maurice huffed.

"Nor I." Claudius drank more beer.

"Well, I do," I replied with conviction and returned my gaze to Sinclaire and Raphael.

We'd had this conversation many times. When Sinclaire came to visit, he didn't just come to see Amelia. He came to see us as a family.

I owed him a lot. He'd made a lot possible for me. If not for him, I'd still be in prison seeing my sentence through with five months left to go.

There'd been no parole mentioned for me probably because that minimum sentence was all they could pin on me. My crimes were so much more severe than the punishment I'd received.

Because of Sinclaire, I'd been able to make it home for my baby's delivery, which ironically was two weeks after I'd been released. Raphael had come early, and I was so happy I'd been there to welcome him into the world and be there for Amelia as she gave birth to him.

So, no matter what, Sinclaire was good in my books. He didn't have to do what he did for me. He never had to. I knew I would always be indebted to him.

Sinclaire picked up Raphael and brought him over to where we sat.

The two were laughing.

Sinclaire handed him to me, and I took my boy

proudly, loving that he put his little arms around my neck.

"That kid gives me a whole month's workout." Sinclaire smiled, taking the seat next to me.

"He'll probably go to sleep now for hours." I brushed my nose over Raphael's tiny one.

"That's good, right?"

"For him."

"So, you guys done talking about me?" Sinclaire looked at Claudius and Maurice.

"No, so much more to say," Claudius answered, resting back against the chair.

"Like what, boss?" Sinclaire chuckled.

Claudius straightened. "Don't call me that. It doesn't suit you, and I would never have you work for me."

I rolled my eyes at him. He was such a prick sometimes, but speaking of who suited what, my brother definitely suited the part of Don to the Chicago mafia.

"Not even if I got you those cigars you like?"

Claudius squinted. "Cough it up, cop, and we'll see."

"Nah, you have to beat me in poker first." Sinclaire smirked.

"You're on."

Just then, the door to the sunroom opened, and Amelia stuck her head out.

A bright smile washed over her face as she looked at me holding Raphael.

"It's Mama, Papa." Raphael beamed, stretching his little hands out to her.

She glided over to us, took him, and gave me a kiss.

"Why is there mud all over the baby?" She winced.

"Blame your boy over there." Maurice pointed his finger at Sinclaire.

"Hey, kids love dirt. Plus, didn't you know a good mud bath is excellent for the skin?" Sinclaire answered with a mischievous smile.

"Bullshit." Claudius smirked.

"Claudius, *language*," Amelia chided.

"Sorry." He smiled. "Bull poop."

Amelia rolled her eyes and looked back to me. "Should we do dinner?"

"Let's. They won't have our amazing food all summer." We were leaving for Italy in a few days. "Maurice, you're up."

Amelia handed Raphael to Maurice.

"Hey, no, my turn." Gigi rushed out the door and took Raphael.

"Unfair, but I won't argue." Maurice chuckled.

"Thank you, dear." Gigi bubbled away, going back into the house with Raphael.

"Happy wife, happy life." Maurice nodded. The two had been married for a year now.

Amelia took my hand and pulled me away from the guys just as Sinclaire laid out his deck of cards.

When we got inside the kitchen, she grabbed a pack of fresh pasta, and I took it from her.

"I'm cooking. You're watching."

"We said *we*." She giggled.

"Yes, so I could have you all to myself."

"So, I'm just going to watch you cook?"

I nodded. "Here's the plan for the evening that I never told you. We cook dinner, Maurice and Gigi are staying over to babysit, and I'm taking you to the ballet later, then to the presidential suite of the Machionette."

"What? Luc, we're leaving for Italy in days. We can't have a break like that and the baby needs us."

"The baby will be fine. Come here." I pulled her closer, and she slipped her arms around me. "Mrs. Morientz, I've only told you once today that I love you."

"Mr. Morientz, you're forgiven, but you have to make up for your severe mistake." She stood on the tips of her toes and kissed me.

"Dinner and dessert."

We both laughed.

"How about dessert first?" She gave me a saucy look.

I loved the sound of that. I loved my life with her. I loved that she gave me a chance to be me.

Most of all, I loved that she loved me.

That was priceless.

Amelia

I walked out into the sea of gardenias covering the front garden of the vineyard. Against the moonlight, they were a stark bright white, like stars kissing the earth.

That was the first thought I'd had on my first visit here last year. I understood what he'd meant every time he used to mention the villa.

The breathtaking image of it was always so striking it gave me goose bumps, and here I was again. Here in the garden in Italy, and the effect was the same.

Maybe a little more because of my deep appreciation for it. I longed to be here when I wasn't, and it was a welcomed break. Most of all, it sparked my creativity.

All I had to do was take a look at the beauty before me, and it channeled the dancer in me, and I'd start seeing dances moves, choreography.

It was amazing how different my life was now. It was so different, sometimes I had a hard time believing everything else that had happened.

It was like I'd always been married to Luc. Like we'd met in high school or something and planned to have the gorgeous wedding we had two years ago, promising our love to each other for all eternity.

It was like we'd always had Raphael. Our precious baby who was a continuous symbol of our love. It was like we'd always planned to name him after my father.

And it was like I'd never left dancing, never left Chicago to become Amelia Taylor, never became someone else.

A month after Raphael was born, I thought I'd take a walk to my old dance school. I'd just wanted to see the place for memory's sake. I was so shocked to find Madame Bouglaise still ran the place and more shocked that she instantly remembered me. That one visit changed everything.

Then sixty-five years old, she'd been looking to sell the school but still have some involvement with the dance examinations and contact with Julliard.

She was the woman who'd practically pruned me and molded me into the dancer I was, so she didn't think twice when I offered to buy the place. Then she made the deal even sweeter with her recommendation to Julliard that I train under her to take on the role of exam liaison officer both at Julliard and the school.

I was accepted under her internship, but on the condition that I did three years training at the undergraduate level and a further year to get the teaching qualification. At Julliard.

Of course, I'd completely agreed to it. My time to dance and travel the world with all the amazing companies I'd hoped to work for might have passed, but that didn't mean I couldn't still live my dream in some way. Teaching was what I'd always planned to do. So it was still me living the dream.

I taught at the school, owned it, and worked closely with one of the best dance academies in the world. It was onwards and upwards from here.

Luc had made it possible. He'd never allowed me to lose sight of my dream.

"You always look the same."

I turned on hearing Luc's voice. He'd been at his office in town working late on the accounts.

When I looked at him sometimes, I couldn't believe he was mine.

In the moonlight, that lit up the vibrant Verona sky, his features looked more chiseled. The angles and planes in his face more pronounced. The bright blue of his eyes became more of a twilight hue in the mingle of light and dark.

He rolled the sleeves up his thick forearms and joined me. That sexy smile of his turning up a notch the more he looked at me.

"The same how?" I ran my fingers across the hard wall of his chest.

"Like the dream I always had of you. Sometimes it's hard to believe this is real, that you're actually here."

"I know the feeling."

His smile widened. He cupped my face and brushed his lips against mine.

"Goddess," he breathed, voice deep and husky. "I want you."

"Take me." I giggled against his lips.

Pressing his lips to mine again, he kissed me until my knees weakened and my whole being felt light, like I might float away.

In a skillful move, he swept me up as if I were

weightless and carried me inside the villa and into our bedroom.

He set me down on the cool wooden floor, and one by one our clothes came off until we were both naked. I giggled when Luc picked me up again and carried me to the massive king-sized bed that filled the space in the center of the room.

I took a moment to admire his gorgeous body. Sleek muscle and untamed pride beamed in the masterpiece he was. Chiseled to perfection, Luc had the body of a warrior. I would never be able to get enough of the rigid contours and planes on his chest and those tattoos.

I loved the power that came from him, but also the beauty.

When he joined me on the bed, his lips recaptured mine, and in a flash, I got sucked into the magic of us. It was divine ecstasy.

Placing me on my back against the cool silk sheets, he traced a sensuous path to ecstasy with his lips right from my mouth, down my neck, the valley between my breasts, down the planes of my stomach, and on to where I craved him most between my thighs.

Passion then fueled the blood through my heart as his expert touching and tasting sent me to higher planes of pleasure. He gave me a wickedly sinful, seductive smile as he slid into me and my body welcomed his. Our bodies in exquisite harmony with each other.

Waves of pleasure and pure delight cascaded over me when he started to move, and my body melted in sweet agony. This was us, always us, existing in this bubble of love where what we did could only be felt by us together riding this magical wave that bound us.

Ours was shared pleasure and like always when we came, it was on a shuddering wave of overwhelming passion that made me dizzy with desire.

Luc lowered his body next to me and pulled me into his arms.

I rested against the corded muscles of his chest, basking in the afterglow of this moment and us.

"Goddess, I can't get enough of you. I don't think I ever will." He whispered against my head. "I want you again."

I smiled and looked up at him. "It's a good thing I want you too, and we have all night."

"All night? No, it's not enough. I think we're going to need a babysitter for the rest of the week." He nodded. The hungry look that lurked in his eyes turned me on even more.

"Yeah, me too."

He reclaimed my lips, giving me a kiss that made my soul shiver and my blood sing through my veins.

I couldn't get enough of this man either.

Thank goodness he was my forever.

That was priceless.

Thank you so much for reading. I won't say it's the end because it's not. Look out for the Gangsters and Dolls series coming soon featuring the stories of Claudius the new Mafia Boss and his men, The Four.

Also coming soon is Hot Pursuit with Sinclaire's story.

ALSO BY KHARDINE GRAY

Other Books by Khardine Gray

Series

The Accidental Mafia Queen

The Vandervilles

Standalones Novels

His Girl Next Door

Blossoms of The Heart

Mr. Delicious

Mailroom Delight

The Rules of Attraction

Falling For Him

Never and Always

I Love You again

One Wild Night

Shape of My Heart

Hearts Entwined

Complete Me

I Only Have Eyes For You

The Objection to Affection

Box Sets

Play of Love

Contains Shape of my Heart, The Road Trip Formerly called One Wild Night and Hearts Entwined.

To check out these titles please visit

https://www.amazon.com/author/khardinegraynovels

ACKNOWLEDGMENTS

To my readers.
Where would I be without you….
This one's for all of you.
I thank you from the bottom of my heart for all
your support, and for reading my stories.
Hugs and LOVE xx

ABOUT THE AUTHOR

Khardine Gray is a USA Today Bestselling author who loves writing sizzling hot contemporary romance, romantic suspense, and paranormal romance.

Her books have sexy, drool-worthy heroes who will make you melt, and sassy, fun loving, ambitious heroines.

She simply adores her readers and loves spoiling them.

Keep up with all her new releases by signing up to her mailing list at http://www.subscribepage.com/f4u3v9